NEW TRICKS

ACE'S WILD, BOOK 10

DAVIDSON KING

resemblance to actual events, locales, or persons, living or dead, is coincidental. All products and/or brand names mentioned are registered trademarks of their respective holders/companies.

ACE'S WILD

Ace's Wild is a multi-author series of books that take place in the same fictional town. Each story can be read in any order. The connecting element in the Ace's Wild series is an adult store owned by Ace and Wilder. The main characters from each book will make at least one visit to Ace's Wild, where they'll buy a toy to use in their story! The only characters who crossover to each book are Ace and Wilder. And with various heat and kink levels, there's sure to be something for everyone!

CHAPTER ONE

Malcolm

"You only have a quarter tank of gas left before you hit empty, Mal. You've decided on a crazy route to my parents' and there's no way of truly knowing when we'll see a gas station again. I did however, see a sign a few miles back for one if you take the next exit. Better to be safe."

It was times like this I had to remind myself I loved Embry Chaisten, my partner of thirteen years. My love for him outweighed the fact he drove me nuts sometimes. He was the order to my chaos, the plan to my spontaneity. Together we oddly made sense. But lately, with the holidays looming, he got worse. His anxiety spiked and with that, his need for order and control took the driver's seat. I knew it even annoyed him sometimes.

"I have a GPS, Em. It tells me where all service stations are, just chill."

His huff made me smile. We were headed down to Belle Isle, Florida, to visit with Embry's parents for Thanksgiving. This would be the first trip we made to see them in five years when Embry and his family had had a huge argument. They'd never been pleased about their son being gay, and when he'd announced he wanted to marry me, it had sent them over the edge. It had ended with unforgivable words that had left thick scars. And we still hadn't tied the knot.

I knew that with every birthday and holiday that had passed Embry by, he'd hoped he would get a call from his parents telling him they were sorry, and they wanted nothing more than for him to marry whomever made him happy. But he just got the generic cards and two-minute calls. I never brought marriage up to him, and I was content with how we loved, but I hated how Embry still let his family hold him back. I think when the invitation to come down for Thanksgiving this year was given, he was hoping this was it. Acceptance.

"You did get this beast serviced before the long drive, right?" He turned toward me, his gorgeous blue eyes sparkling, yet nervous. The sun glinted perfectly, making the auburn and golden streaks of his hair almost glow.

"I did."

"You didn't ask your friend Zell, did you? I researched him and I was right, no licenses, nothing." He tsked and shook his head.

"No, I didn't ask Zell to do it. I went to the mechanic by your work, remember? You picked me up when I dropped off my Land Rover."

I peeked over at him and found him looking out the window. He didn't answer me, just scrunched his nose and shrugged. When Embry felt out of his element, he got defensive. I often called him out on it, but I knew sometimes you had to let things go. He was likely a mess in that brilliant head of his.

I never wanted to go to Belle Isle for Thanksgiving. I wanted to stay in Queens and have the holidays with my very loving, very inclusive, very non-conservative family. My mother had a way with Embry, and my dad thought he was hilarious. Not that

Embry intended to be funny, my dad just thought he was. We were a huge family with my four brothers and two sisters, and we supported each other. Completely opposite to the Chaistens.

Embry's father had also made it known that he considered Embry being a teacher less than. Embry enjoyed teaching high school history. He lit up when he told me about a student who finally got something he'd been trying to drill into their head for weeks. He loved his job and he couldn't even share that with his family.

His mother wasn't much better. She'd never stood up for her son and had a sneer that would freeze fire in its place. Her opinions were cutting to everything Embry was as a person. When they'd called three weeks ago and told Embry they missed him and asked him to give them another chance, he'd clung to it. I didn't want to go, but I knew Embry loved his family in his own way and I wanted to support him. The condition was that we drove there and didn't fly. I thought it would give Embry time to calm down and maybe have a small adventure.

"How long have we been in the car? Feels like a million hours," Embry said as we passed another exit.

"Just over two hours since we finished lunch. Good thing you teach history and not math." I chuckled when Embry rolled his eyes at me good-naturedly. It was about a sixteen-hour drive to Embry's folks, but we agreed to do it in two days so we wouldn't show up at an ungodly hour. There was no chance in hell I was staying with Embry's parents, so I'd booked a room at the nearest hotel to their house. I figured I'd tell Embry when we got closer to Belle Isle.

"We should stop soon. I need to call my mother and let her know we're on schedule. She'll be grateful for the update." I knew he was saying that more for his own benefit than mine—convincing himself she'd want to know.

"I'm the one driving, go ahead and call her while we're on the road."

His head whipped in my direction and I wanted to laugh at his expression. I was sure it scared his students, but I just thought he was adorable.

"Mal, you know how unsteady a call is if we're moving! The call could drop and then my mother would think I hung up and…"

"And you'd have to call her back and say you didn't? If you think she wouldn't understand a dropped call, then you're not ready for this visit, Em."

He released a sigh, his shoulders sagged, and I knew he was wound tight. He needed a break.

"How about this, we'll stop closer to the ocean, have some coffee, maybe pie?" I winked knowing it was a weakness of his. "You can call her and let her know, and then we'll drive a few more hours before breaking for the night. Sound good?"

"It's a plan?" He asked because I didn't do plans. I was a fly-by-the-seat-of-my-pants kind of guy. But plans made Embry feel grounded.

"Yeah, Em, a plan." I pulled over and checked the map on my GPS. "Okay, let's head toward Raleigh. We just have forty-five minutes to get there. Then we'll drive closer to the shore and you can call your mom. We'll have been driving for over eight hours by then and we'll both appreciate a bed."

Em nodded, pleased with the plan, and his body immediately relaxed. I put the new destination into the GPS and pulled back onto the highway. Worrying about Embry's parents exhausted him. I wished he'd let me deal with things more. He had to have his order and his way, but his way wasn't working, especially lately. Sometimes I wished I could push his boundaries and help him let go. Show him how freeing and amazing it could be to just go with the flow for a bit.

I'd need some sort of a miracle to put a plan like that into action. Of course, I should be careful what I wished for; karma had a funny way of helping a guy out. We had just passed a sign that said Welcome to Vintage Ridge when there was a horrible sound coming from the car, followed by smoke, and a clang and a crash.

"What the hell?" Embry shouted.

My Land Rover bucked and then like a switch turned off, it stopped.

"Damn." I hit the steering wheel in frustration and dared to look over at Embry. His eyes narrowed and his lips were thinned out. His beautiful pale skin began to turn a lovely shade of red, and when he opened his mouth, I waited.

"You did take it to Zell to service it, didn't you?"

"No! I took it to the place you recommended and look what happened." I gestured to the lightly smoking hood of the car.

"Sure, blame me. I suggested the place, I expected you to do your research, Mal." He folded his arms over his chest and glared at me.

"I'll call our roadside assistance. Maybe now would be a good time to call your mom and tell her there may be a delay." I hopped out of the car to make my call without waiting to hear Embry's reply. I loved him and I understood him, but sometimes, it was best if I stepped away.

Luckily, roadside assistance said there was a service station in the town we had just entered and I took the time, while I watched Embry through the windshield talking to his mother, to order an Uber.

I couldn't for the life of me understand what happened to the car, but judging from his expression, I knew whatever the mechanic told me was going to be less painful than what Embry's mother was saying to him right now.

CHAPTER TWO

Embry

"Oh, Embry, that's just horrid. I don't understand why you chose to drive such a long distance and not fly." My mother huffed and I would have said something, but I knew she wasn't done.

"That Malcolm always has to do things the hard way, his way. It's some sort of macho posturing if you ask me. Seriously, Embry, there has to be an airport nearby, simply fly here and Malcolm will take care of things. I want to see my son for Thanksgiving."

Margaret Chaisten, my mother, made no secret of her dislike for Malcolm. She'd never seen what I saw in him and she'd never even tried. Even though this was one of her tamer ways of implying she didn't think he needed to be with us for Thanksgiving, it was still a loud suggestion.

"I'm not leaving Malcolm here to deal with the car and miss Thanksgiving with him." I could see Malcolm pacing in front of the Land Rover. It wasn't smoking anymore, so I knew he was out there to give me privacy.

"But you're okay with not being with me on Thanksgiving?" Her voice rose an octave or two and this time I huffed.

"Do you even hear yourself, Mother? Would you leave Father? No, you wouldn't. I can't even believe you suggested it." After the blow up five years ago, I stuck up for myself more with my family when we talked. I knew my parents likely found it a victory—for them—since Mal and I hadn't married yet, but some part of me craved them saying okay to the union. I knew in my heart that was what I was waiting for. Those words, that they gave their blessing. I was hoping that would happen this holiday, and then we'd get married in the spring or summer.

"I'm sorry, Embry. I miss you so much I got carried away. Of course, you wouldn't leave Malcolm. You're a sensible person."

The lights from the tow truck became visible over the small hill. "I have to go, Mother. The tow truck is here and Mal and I have to figure out accommodations for the evening. I'll call you when I have more information."

"Very well. Speak soon." No goodbye or I love you, just a click. I took a deep breath, swallowing down the hurt I felt at her dismissal.

I saw the large tow truck driver approach Mal with his arm out and hand open for a shake, then they were talking, likely about the car since Mal gestured to it a few times. Mal wasn't a small man, far taller than me and well built, but this man was like a giant grizzly bear with a megawatt smile. After a minute or two, I stepped out of the car to hear what they were saying.

"Oh boy, you got yourself in a bit of a mess, huh?" He looked at Mal then me. "Hey there, I'm Foreman. Malcolm here just told me what happened."

"Yes. I'm Embry Chaisten. Do you have any idea how long this will take to repair? We're on our way to Florida for Thanksgiving and—"

Foreman cut me off with a booming laugh. "Oh, I've never

been to Florida. I want to take my girl to The Epcot place, maybe." He shrugged.

"Just Epcot, or Epcot Center. Not The Epcot," I corrected him, earning a glare from Mal, and immediately feeling shitty for correcting him. "But that's a good name too, I like it."

Foreman laughed again. "Well, Embry Chaisten, I can't tell you the repair timing until I get under this lady's skirt." I tilted my head not understanding what he was talking about. Foreman must've sensed I had no idea and patted the hood of the car, making it clear the lady, was in fact, the car.

"I ordered an Uber. They'll drive us into town and we'll stay at a hotel there."

"The Vintage Hotel is a nice place for you fine folks. Helen runs it; tell her I sent you. I can call over there in the morning when I know more about the car."

"Thank you, Foreman," Mal said and shook the big man's hand once more.

We stood off to the side while Foreman got the Land Rover chained up, and as he was about to go, the Uber arrived.

"Hey there. So, headed to the Vintage Hotel?" the Uber driver asked.

"Yes. On the map it just said VRH. We're unfamiliar with the area, so I'm glad I hit the right place. Thanks."

The driver nodded. "Not a problem."

We were quiet for a few minutes while the driver smoothly navigated us toward civilization. We passed a few small places, and I could admit the town was quaint, but I hated the unfamiliar feeling I got in the pit of my stomach. I didn't like new anything.

"What's that?" Mal asked, and I turned to look out his window. There was a brick building with a white sign that read Ace's Wild.

"There's handcuffs on the letters. Perhaps it's a uniform store for the authorities," I answered. It seemed the most logical, I mean…

My thoughts were shattered when the driver laughed loudly. "Sorry, dude, don't mean to laugh at you. I thought maybe it was a joke." He made eye contact with me through the mirror. "But you weren't kidding so, yeah, oops."

"What is that place, then?" I asked, not enjoying being laughed at.

"Ace's Wild is an adult store. Ace and Wilder run it, great guys. Born and raised right here in Vintage Ridge. Left for a time but came back ready to spread the word of love through sex positivity."

I could feel my eyes widening. Mal was being really quiet and I looked over at him. We'd passed the store, but he was still gazing out the window.

"What's on your mind, Mal?" I asked as I gently squeezed his shoulder. I didn't like when he got quiet. He was the boisterous one, the one to take charge of most social situations. I had no more interest in talking with the rude driver and wanted Mal to take over.

"We should go there," he said, and for a moment, I was lost until I realized what he was saying.

"To the sex shop?" I chuckled. "That's not really our thing."

He shrugged and turned toward me. His honey brown eyes sparkled with mischief. It was the very same look he gave me when he asked me out all those years ago. "We're stuck in this town for at least a day or two, let's make it a real adventure."

"You think whipping me would be an adventure I'd like?" I raised a brow and laughed. "Not my scene, Mal."

"It's more than whips and chains in adult shops, Em."

"You know this how?"

He huffed and ran his fingers through his short hair. "I've researched things. I—" his gaze flitted to the driver, who was doing a poor job of not eavesdropping. "I think it'll be good for you."

"Me?" I said louder than I would've liked. "What's that supposed to mean?"

"I just, look, what if I make you a deal?"

My eyes narrowed and I could admit, I was intrigued. "What kind of deal?"

His smile was brilliant and I knew I'd never tire of it. "You let me get two, maybe three toys and we experiment a little. I think you'll love it, but if you don't—" He closed his eyes as if he was going to regret what he was going to say. "I will let you plan our entire vacation this summer."

Mal hated plans. He despised having his free time scheduled. I, on the other hand, thrived on order. For him to give into this without a fight was huge.

"Three toys maximum, we experiment only for the time we're here in this town, and if I hate it, I get to plan our vacation?"

"Yes."

"And what if I love it?" I had a feeling I wouldn't, but I liked to know all the facts before making a decision.

"If you love it, then we do it again, and we explore it together and maybe you'll find out things are fun on the kinkier side."

I glanced at the driver who wore a huge smile and was nodding.

"Okay, Mal, you have a deal."

CHAPTER THREE

Malcolm

EMBRY WASN'T A DARING SORT OF GUY. HE WAS THE ERR-ON-THE-side-of-caution guy. I saw him talking to his mother through the car window and knew she was pissing him off. If I was a betting man, I'd say she was trying to convince Em to leave me and fly to her. But he'd never do it, even if I told him to. He loved me and I loved him.

When the driver said Ace's Wild was an adult store, it was like all the pieces aligned and the idea struck. I didn't need whips, floggers, or anything like that. I had, in fact, researched after I'd mentioned to a friend how tight Embry was wound, and how I wished I could help him relax more. They'd referenced a few sites on the internet—from lighter kink to BDSM—and soon I was looking them up and immersing myself in their knowledge.

Embry got lost in his head. He was afraid to let go because by doing so, he had no control and that was everything to him. He needed to see that relinquishing it was not only safe, but it was freeing.

"Thanks, man," I said to the driver as he dropped us in front of the hotel. "Let's check in and then we can head on over to that store. It doesn't seem far, so we can walk it."

"Walk it?" His gaze shifted all over, and he began wringing his hands together. The town was one of the most non-threatening I'd ever been in, but Em didn't like the unknown.

"It's a nice evening, not too cold. It's like half a mile, max. Then we can grab some food if we see a place and come back here for some fun." I winked, glad to see his cheeks pinken up.

"Okay, Mal. I'm really going to enjoy planning our vacation." He chuckled, his hands slipping into his pockets, and I followed him inside.

Foreman was right, Helen was truly lovely and sympathetic to our situation. She said she had a room and even told us about a few places that were still open if we wanted to get toiletries and such.

"Oh, dangit. We left our luggage in the car," Embry said after Helen was through telling us about the stores.

"Not to worry, dear. I'll call Foreman and have him bring them by. Let's get you settled in your room first, and he'll will bring them over soon."

"Thank you so much, Helen. Can you bring them inside when they arrive? Embry and I are going to take a walk and explore the town," I said as we followed her to the elevator.

"Okay." She smiled, and when we got to the floor, she handed us the keycard. "It's the second door on the left. If you need anything, dial one on the phone."

"Thanks, Helen." I smiled and Embry nodded and began moving toward the room quickly.

"I hope they change the sheets more than once a week here," he said as I slipped the card in and the little light turned green.

"This place is clean and well maintained, Em. I'm sure Helen takes good care of it."

We stepped inside and it was exactly how I thought it would

be. It felt like home. Cream colored carpets and drapes. The sofa was a rose gold, and there was a set of French doors that no doubt led to the bedroom. It had a tiny kitchen with just a sink and small fridge. No stove, but there was a microwave. A cherry wood desk was against the wall, and the two windows were floor to ceiling. It was gorgeous.

"It looks nice," Embry said as he brushed a hand over the upholstery of the sofa. "I'll check the bedroom."

I followed behind, smiling when I heard him gasp. The bed was made of oak and had crisp white sheets. That wasn't what made him gasp. It was the canopy with white silks draped over it, giving the feeling of being whisked away in the clouds.

"Looks like Foreman was right," I said as I rested my hands on Em's shoulders. "Place is perfect for folks like us, huh?"

He hummed and rested against my chest. With this minor surrender, there was a fluttering in the pit of my stomach, making me wonder how amazing his full submission would be. Just knowing we were going to do this made it impossible for me not to think about it.

We cleaned up as best we could and left the hotel for the walk to Ace's Wild. I hoped our bags were at the hotel when we returned. I wanted to start our evening with washing Embry from head to toe.

As we walked down the street, hand in hand, there weren't any sneers, no one even seemed to notice. Living in New York there was a huge amount of acceptance, but we'd gone to many small towns where Embry and my affections were met with disgust. I hadn't been sure what to expect from Vintage Ridge, so I was relieved to see it so accepting. It was dark out now, but the streetlights illuminated the area perfectly. I was surprised by how busy the night was in such a peaceful town.

"I smell snow in the air," Embry said as puffs of white smoke flowed from his mouth.

"Hopefully it'll hold off until we're out of here. Though, driving in snow is no big deal for me. I'll do it if I have to." I shrugged and when the sign said we could walk, we hastily made it across the street.

I felt Embry's hand squeeze mine tightly as the sign for Ace's Wild shone in the night. For me, it was a beacon to a new beginning, for Embry, I had no doubt, it was a light of doom. I hated how his anxiety ruled his everyday life, and I knew how he tried to overcome so much and not let it dictate him. Embry often told me how his father always looked down on new and innovative things. From a young age, Embry feared change because it always came with insult and humiliation from the man. I'd spent years trying to encourage change in Embry's life, and every so often, I saw a glimmer of hope.

"Looks non-threatening, don't you think?" I nudged his shoulder, but he didn't say anything. His mouth was set in a line, and he probably had a million thoughts running through his head.

We opened the doors to the store and were welcomed with two things: a warmth that thawed the early winter chill and booming laughter.

"I don't see anything wrong with putting a naked Santa up on the roof," a voice filled with joy said. Embry and I turned to see a large black man carrying a very naked Santa doll and a frustrated shorter man, his complete opposite, trailing behind.

"In the store, yes; up on the roof for all to see, even children, no, Ace!" the shorter man said as he pushed his glasses up his nose. The shorter one was adorable, really. He reminded me of a slightly older Embry in a lot of ways. He was also making the big man laugh as he tried to pry naked Santa from his hands.

"Oh, come on, Wilder. It'll make people come in. Come in… get it?"

"No," the shorter man, Wilder, said. He held up a finger to Ace and was trying to stifle a laugh. "Bad joke."

At that, I couldn't hold back my own laughter. This, of course, made both men turn to see Embry and I, hand in hand, staring at them.

"Naked Santa, right?" the larger man asked as he held up the inflatable Santa doll and of course, at that moment, the inflatable penis flagged.

"Oh, that's just a sad state to be in," Embry said, which made the two men laugh right away. I was shocked he made such an uncharacteristic comment, especially knowing how nervous he was, but the smirk on Embry's face and the situation itself had me laughing a moment later.

CHAPTER FOUR

Embry

I was aware I was in an adult store, but the sight before me made it feel more like a comedy act. As soon as the laughter died down, a man approached us. The bigger gentleman called him Wilder, and I was surprised and impressed with his appearance. He reminded me a little of myself. He adjusted his glasses and held up his hand.

"Good evening, I'm Wilder, part owner, and this guy behind me is Ace, the other owner and my, at times, better half."

I felt my eyes widen. With one so prim and put together, and the other more wild looking in a teddy bear kind of way, they couldn't be more opposite. So much like… Oh. Just like me and Malcolm.

"Pardon my better half." Malcolm winked at me. "I'm Mal and this is Embry. We're unexpectedly passing through since our car died. Saw this place on our way to the hotel and wanted to check it out."

"Out of towners!" Ace shouted as he dropped Santa. "Where you from?"

We talked for a few about where we were from and where we were headed, and while Mal talked seamlessly with the men, I took in the scenery of the store. Sexual contraptions in all shapes and sizes hung on racks, walls, and mannequins; some had spikes, others were leather. Honestly, some appeared to be very uncomfortable. There were themed dildos, and one that claimed to cheer when you climaxed. I didn't know half of what I was looking at, but I had a niggling fear as to what Mal was going to do to me.

"First time?" Wilder whispered for only me to hear. Ace and Mal seemed to be embracing some newfound bromance and ignoring us.

"Am I so obvious?"

He nodded. "We have a lot of curious people come in. We always advise them to start small. Don't grab a cane and clamps and walk out like you're a pro. Am I wrong to assume you aren't just here for some lube or condoms?"

"No, you're right. I go to the regular store for that stuff." I chuckled nervously. Wilder just smiled peacefully, instantly calming me.

Ace and Mal had quieted, so Wilder addressed us both.

"Kink isn't a one-way thing. There's no bar you need to stand on. It's personal, and it's no one else's place to judge what makes it work for the two of you. Embry here tells me you're new to this. Can I help you find anything?"

I held my breath, worried Mal might go a more advanced route but he didn't, not even a little.

"I'm looking for a blindfold, soft restraints, and perhaps a feather tickler? I read up on some things and for what I have in mind, I think those will be perfect."

Wilder and Ace wore matching smiles. "I'm thrilled to hear you did some research, and it sounds like you're beginning well. Right this way." Mal and I followed Wilder, while Ace picked up

Santa and said he had to see about finding a plug for him. I did not ask further questions.

Twenty minutes later, we were walking out of the store with a bag filled with toys. Mal's smile was huge, and I was still nervous, but nothing of what he bought was terrifying. He didn't fantasize about jumping into anything too far beyond our normal sex life, and with each step, I felt the tingling of anticipation. But there was no way in hell I was going to tell him that.

"Hungry?" Mal asked as we came up to a restaurant. It looked like a pub of some sort. Through the window I could see that it wasn't busy which made me happy.

"I could eat."

He held the door open and I stepped in. It was an Irish pub with round wooden tables, a large bar, and the smell of fried foods and alcohol. It reminded me of one of those places Mal loved to go with his friends for Sunday football. It had a certain amount of familiarity to it.

"You can sit anywhere," a woman carrying a tray said as she passed. "I'll bring menus over in a sec."

I chose a far-off table in the corner by the window. It afforded us privacy so people couldn't see what Mal was carrying, but we had enough of a view outside that we could watch people passing by.

"I could eat a horse," Mal said as he placed the bag on an empty seat, and then his eyes met mine. They twinkled with joy and I loved the light he gave out. I knew I wasn't an easy man to love and I'd said that to Mal many times. He'd shake his head and tell me it was because I couldn't see what he did. No one had ever made the noise in my head go away like Mal. He made me want to be a better person and never once looked at me like I was crazy. He made my heart beat faster with just a smile, and when he hugged me, all my shattered pieces melded together. He reached across the table and took my hands.

"You okay, Em?"

"I am. Just, a lot on my mind, you know?"

He didn't get a chance to respond since the waitress came over and placed menus down. I ordered a ginger-ale and Mal ordered a large water. Neither of us were drinkers, and for tonight, I really didn't want to be impaired.

"Oh, burgers," Mal said with a chuckle. That man loved his red meat. I couldn't help but laugh at the joy he found in beef.

When the waitress came back, Mal ordered his burger with everything.

"How about you, hon?" She smiled.

"I'd like the butter chicken, but please, no cilantro; instead of fries, can I have a salad with a low-fat balsamic dressing, and is there any way to have the tomatoes in the salad removed, please?"

She stared at me. I always hated when I had to make special requests about food and people looked at me like I was a pain in the ass. It wasn't my intention, and I always said please. I had particular tastes, and so many times, I wanted to say nevermind and just fix the dish when it was served.

"Of course she can, right?" Mal said as he leaned across the table and rubbed over my fingers with his hand and smiled. "Not hard requests."

This was reason twenty-seven why I loved Mal. No matter how silly or insane my requests were, he backed me up, every time.

"Sure." Her eyebrows rose as she wrote it down. "It'll be out soon."

After the waitress was gone, I asked Mal if he was going to at least tell me what he was planning for later.

"No. But you have to understand that me not telling you is actually part of the plan." He released a breath. "You have to trust me, Em."

"You know I do, I just…"

"Have a hard time letting things go and letting others be in charge."

I nodded. "Yes."

"I will say that before we begin we'll need to talk about a few things, but I don't want to do it here out in the open." He scanned the room, no one was paying us any mind, but I appreciated not discussing it further here.

"Fair enough."

Our food came out, and we fell into a comfortable silence as we ate. My chicken was delicious, and I cleared my plate, as did Mal. As nervous as I was—which was a common feeling for me —I managed to always eat and take care of myself.

We paid the check, and bag in hand, we walked back to the hotel. Helen smiled and told us our bags had arrived and asked if we needed anything else.

"No, thank you, Helen. Embry and I are going to get some rest. We'll see you in the morning."

"Very well, goodnight, boys." She smiled and eyed the bag. Heat rushed to my cheeks. *Great, now Helen is going to know we're getting freaky in the bedroom.*

I must have been fidgeting or something because when we entered our hotel room, Mal dropped the bag on the chair and wrapped me in his arms.

"Breathe, Em. It's me. Nothing I ever do to you will hurt you. I love you and only want to make you fly." His voice was so calming. I wanted to shout at him, yell that there were worse things than physical pain. But he rocked me back and forth in his large protective arms, and the words lost their sharpness.

"I know you'd never hurt me, Mal. It's more than that sometimes, though. Sometimes the things I fear aren't physical. Flying sounds terrifying. It's letting go, not having control."

I felt him nod against me. "We have to talk. There's still control you can have in this."

I lifted my head and stared into his warm eyes. "How?"

"Let's take a bath, relax, and we can talk more about tonight."

I followed him into the bathroom in silence, waiting for the butterflies in my stomach to chill out. As the bathroom filled with steam and the scent of sandalwood and lavender, I started to calm.

Mal's face held a promise I wanted to claim, so with a small smile, I began to strip.

CHAPTER FIVE

Malcolm

I SAT ON THE EDGE OF THE TUB TRANSFIXED WHILE EMBRY confidently removed his clothes. I'd seen him naked hundreds of times but for some reason this, tonight, felt like the first. He wasn't just stripping the layers of clothes, this was his way of saying he was ready and trusted me.

He was gorgeous to me no matter what. Neither one of us were perfect or flawless. He had a scar where his appendix was removed when he was ten, his legs were slightly skinny, and I always chuckled at his pinky on his left hand. It was like it got tired of growing and stopped right before the finish line. But to me, Embry was perfect. Imperfectly so.

He removed his glasses and placed them beside the sink, and when his blue eyes peered up at me, it stole my breath.

"I'll never get tired of looking at you."

He smiled bigger this time and rewarded me with a little hip wiggle as he unbuttoned his pants. And within a minute, he was completely naked.

"Your turn," he whispered.

I wasn't going to linger, if it took me two minutes to be completely bare that was stretching it. He chuckled as I opened my arms in a ta-da gesture.

"How about we get in the tub and we can talk," I said as I offered my hand.

When I had Embry's back against my chest, ensconced in my arms, I softly began to talk to him.

"I don't know how much you know about types of kink, Em, so stop me or whatever as I'm talking." He nodded, so I continued.

"I don't know a lot, only what interested me and what I thought would be something you maybe, at some point, might want to try. I researched everything, so I'm not suggesting we jump into anything hardcore. Maybe softer kink in a sense. To be honest, I was trying to find ways to help you relax and this is what I found." It felt like I was rambling, but Embry understood me. He often said he spoke Mal.

"I'm not feeling like this is going to be very relaxing," he said with a chuckle.

"No, I get that, but I feel like what I have in mind is something you'll respond to well."

Embry's body had been stiff, but with my explanation, he immediately relaxed. One thing I could say is that the years had taught me how to read Embry well.

"We've known each other for so many years, and the last few have been the toughest for you. I watched you work yourself practically to death just to grasp some semblance of control. I know you love your family, but they're a chaos in your life you can't tame. It's led you to massive anxiety, stress, panic, and discomfort. You're disconnected and can't find your outlet. I feel, I really and truly feel, I can help you find it."

Embry released a breath and I could sense he was trying to

find the right words, so I stayed silent for a little while to give him time.

"Mal?"

"Yeah?"

"I don't know that I do love my family."

I had to work at not letting Embry feel my body practically jump at that revelation. "Why?"

"It's not something I always felt. And a part of me feels horrible inside for feeling it. But tonight, talking to my mother, I realized she's never going to love you, love us. She'll fight me tooth and nail and my family will back her. How can I love people who don't love me back? I mean yeah—" Embry paused to circle himself in my arms so we were now facing each other "—I think they love just me. The Embry they raised. But they really love the Embry they thought they trained."

"That's a lot to hold on to, Em." He nodded and reached for the washcloth, which I took out of his hand. "Let me wash you." He didn't fuss and let me. I watched his face. He was so lost in his head.

"Love comes in so many different forms, Em. I know it's hard to love people who don't love you in return. Harder when they actually think they do love you." I sighed at the confusing explanation. "But not loving them because they can't like me, is it worth it?"

Without hesitation, Em answered, "Yes. Because you're my everything, Mal. You're my north, my yang, my oxygen. They should love you because you center me and adore me unconditionally. But they don't because they'd rather me be with someone who fits their views. And that's not loving me, Mal, that's changing me."

I dropped the washcloth into the water, then reached out and cupped Embry's face in my hands. "You know tonight isn't about me changing you, right?"

He smiled, eyes darting to my lips. "Yeah, Mal, I know."

Leaning forward I pressed my damp lips to his, my body coming alive as his tongue tenderly tried to push into my mouth. I let him have this last moment of control and opened for him. Kissing Embry was like salvation. Nothing mattered here but us, and before we broke apart, I silently promised to love him no matter if this night was a disaster or a success. I'd always give him what he needed because whatever he needed I wanted.

"Even though I said it's a softer side of kink, and I'd never do anything more if you asked me to stop. Do you think you want a safe word since we're doing something so new?" I asked, grabbing the washcloth once again and washing his body.

"Like red, yellow, that sort of thing?" he asked as I made circles on his chest with soapy water.

"We could stick to those sorts of words. Do you get what each means?"

He rolled his eyes which was endearing. "Yes, I do watch television and read books. Just because I've never been in the BDSM lifestyle or anything doesn't mean I'm not knowledgeable in the lingo."

Chuckling, I continued to soap his body. "I think since you're familiar with those we should use them. How's that sound?"

I could tell he was thinking it over, like he does everything, and then he nodded. "Sounds fine to me." He stood, water flowing down his naked pale skin in rivets. "Let's drain the water and shower this soap off."

We spent the next twenty minutes simply washing and talking about the pub and town. It was a nice place to visit. I wasn't sure I could live without the hustle and bustle I was so used to, but I'd definitely come back here.

When we were dried off, we stood in the middle of the bedroom. The oak bed with its stark white sheets beckoned us. I felt the pull and while Embry's face was a perfect pink due to nerves, his cock was half-mast. He was excited.

"Em, it's us, okay? Mal and Em, just us." He nodded. "But when I say get on the bed, we're beginning and I'm going to take control of your pleasure, and unless you use your safe words, you have to do as I say. This is about you not thinking, and trusting me to take care of you. Do you understand?"

Embry's smile was almost shy. I knew this was the most difficult thing for him, relinquishing control, but I also knew my Embry was desperate to quiet the chaos in his head.

"Okay, Mal, you're the boss."

I took a deep breath and said the words that would start this night, and hopefully, be the beginning of something amazing.

"Get on the bed."

CHAPTER SIX

Embry

I CLIMBED UP ONTO THE BED, WHICH WAS REALLY PRETTY magnificent. The sheets were soft, the mattress exactly what I'd choose to sleep on. As I sprawled on my back and stared up at the canopy with its thin white fabrics, it felt like a dream. Like this wasn't happening, but I didn't want to wake up because I really wanted it to be real. It was such a long way from my thoughts on Mal's idea a mere three hours ago.

"I'm going to get you out of that head of yours," Mal's voice grumbled close to my ear. I turned and his honey eyes were smiling at me.

"I look forward to seeing you try." I smiled when he shook his head. He turned toward the nightstand, and the Ace's Wild bag was right there. He removed a feather tickler thing, soft restraints, and a blindfold. All things I would normally never want near me.

"I'm going to start with restraining your arms." He gazed at me, fierce determination shone there now. "If you fight me, I will tie your legs." I wasn't ready for the shiver that passed through me, but I could admit I liked it.

I was speechless as I watched him take the soft black restraints and put one on each wrist. There was a somewhat thick strap that allowed them to tie together and I wondered what Mal would do. He couldn't tie me to each post since it was a king-sized bed and I wasn't elastic.

He smiled beatifically and climbed onto the bed. He straddled me and his gorgeous cock dangled over my torso as he wrapped the strap once around my wrists then lifted them over my head.

"There's this ornate thing here on the headboard, perfect to tie you to." He chuckled, and when he leaned up more, the head of his cock brushed my face, and I couldn't help but lick the glistening pre-come that was there.

He jolted back and glared. "No touching, Em. If I want my dick sucked, I'll make you suck it. Understand me?"

Hot damn, this Mal was going to have me coming before he even touched me. "Okay, Mal."

His features softened. "Are we still good?"

I nodded. "Green."

He moved back up to make sure my wrists were secure. He slipped a finger between the material and my skin to be sure he wasn't cutting off circulation. I was very impressed. Once he was happy with his handiwork, his fingers lightly brushed down my arms. He still straddled me but took his time touching my arms, shoulders, chest, and nipples. I felt them pebble beneath his touch and released a shuddering breath.

"I'm gonna kiss you, Em." I didn't know why he was saying that, he never… "Everywhere. There's not going to be an inch of your flesh that doesn't meet my lips and my tongue."

Fucking Christ. "Um, yeah, okay, sounds… lovely."

He chuckled. "The point of this is to focus on me. What I'm doing, how it makes you feel."

"I have no doubt it'll feel amazing, Mal."

He pressed a soft kiss against my mouth. "It will." He lifted up and smiled sweetly. "To truly focus on me I'm going to take away your sight."

He removed his hand and I spoke, "Why?"

"When a sense is removed the others work harder. Each acts as a crutch for the other. You're the type of person who thrives on visual knowledge. You need to process things that way, and it's also been something that has worked against you. You see it, you believe it." He pinched one of my nipples, making me yelp.

"So wouldn't that mean I need that?"

He shook his head. "No, Em. It means you rely on seeing to believe. Now I want you to feel and trust. Focus on me, my touch. Wonder where I'll go next. Make your only thought in that tornado brain of yours be me and you."

What could I say? He made sense and I couldn't argue the facts. "You're the boss."

"Also—" he reached for the blindfold "—no speaking from this point on unless it's to safe word or I ask you a question."

"But that's…" He covered my mouth again.

"Em, I need you to try and trust me."

I didn't say anything and he smiled. He placed one hand behind my head to lift it so he could get the strap there. Right before he placed the blindfold over my eyes, he kissed me.

"I love you, Em."

I wanted to say it back, and by the expression on his face he knew I did, but I couldn't because it would be breaking the rules. He did love me, but he was testing me.

In the next second, everything went dark. All I felt was him still straddling me, and I heard my pulse in my ears. This was harder than I thought it would be. I didn't realize how much I relied on my sight to take the world in.

"Still good?" Mal asked, and just the sound of his voice calmed me.

"Green."

"Good." I felt the weight of his body lift, and the vulnerable feeling of him not being there spiked my heart rate. *Did he leave?*

"I'm right here, Em. Focus."

The light feeling of his lips began at my toes. I'd never been a person who had a foot fetish. As a matter of fact, I found feet to be disgusting. But in that moment, as Mal kissed each toe, grazed his tongue over them, I wasn't feeling grossed out. It was a pleasant sensation.

I could feel my body relaxing as Mal practically made love to my feet. Not knowing each time his kisses or licks halted, where they'd be felt next, was a little unnerving.

He moved his way up to my ankles, and who the hell knew that was an erogenous zone? I hoped the moan that escaped my mouth wouldn't be against his rules.

"I want to hear how this pleases you, Em. Those are the noises I do want."

As his fingers trailed over my shins and calves, followed by his plush lips and heavenly tongue, I let those sounds fly free. I wanted to beg him to fuck me, suck me. I wanted to tell him to just do it. And that realization was like a lightning strike. I couldn't. I had to obey him. Give him my surrender.

As Mal moved higher, ever so slowly, my mind started drifting. Not out of boredom or irritation, but because of Mal. It was electric how much each caress, every kiss or lick, sparked something inside me. I anticipated where he'd go and wasn't always right. I wanted to grab him and smash my lips to his, and at the same time, I wanted him to calm the storm that raged inside my head.

CHAPTER SEVEN

Malcolm

I COULD DO THIS TO EMBRY ALL NIGHT. HE WAS MORE responsive to me than ever before. Sex had always been amazing with him, but this? It was almost magical. His flesh was covered in goosebumps, his nipples were pebbled, and his cock was so hard pre-come was dripping onto his stomach. I wanted to taste him, but I was taking my time. I'd edge him and have him shaking with need before I took him. I eyed the feather tickler but chose not to use it. I wondered if Embry was thinking I would, and that made me decide to use it another time.

By the time I reached his thighs and hips, he was whimpering, and it was a beautiful sound. I licked over his hip bones and dragged my lips over to the crevice between his leg and his cock.

"You want me so badly." I hummed against his skin. I knew forcing him not to speak had to be killing him, but I had a feeling he was also loving it.

"You taste incredible." I skirted my tongue around his cock, only letting my breath dance over his needy flesh.

"One more thing I should've mentioned." I smiled when he

stilled his writhing body. "You can't come until I say so." His groan was one of frustration, massive horniness, and I knew he wanted to yell at me.

I blew lightly over the damp tip of his dick, smiling when it twitched and Embry's hums became almost frantic.

"Want me to suck you?" I asked, allowing him to answer the question.

"Fuck, yes, Mal, I want you to suck me, damn it, please!" He stretched that answer out as far as he could, and I wanted to tell him one word answers next time but witnessing how passionate he was in this moment, how sex crazed and free he looked, I wanted all his trembling, wanting words.

Feather light, my tongue licked up his balls to the top of his cock. Embry arched up desperately trying to chase the sensation, but I wasn't going to make it so easy for my stubborn and bossy man.

I teased and edged him until I lost track of time. He was mumbling incoherently, so I stayed focused on his body and cues. Around the fifth, maybe sixth, time of staving off his orgasm, I thought Embry was going to scream. But he didn't. I held the base of his shaft and looked at him while removing the blindfold. There was no anger there, no frustration that would lead to a screaming match. There was total and complete adoration. His eyes sparkled and his gaze was synonymous with a daydream.

I released him, and keeping eye contact, reached to the night-stand for the lube. Embry's breathing was surprisingly steady, but the sweat that beaded on his skin told me how much of a ride I'd given him so far.

"Hey, baby," I whispered. "You're so beautiful like this." His hum was like the most perfect musical note. "I'm going to let you come now. You want that?"

"Yes." His answer was breathless.

With lube in hand, I moved between his legs, bending and

spreading them so I could see his perfect hole. Gently I brushed a finger over it, smiling when it winked and Embry moaned.

"Okay, baby. Hang on a little longer. Once I'm inside you, come anytime."

I squirted the lube on my bare cock. Embry and I hadn't used protection for years and the thought of any barrier between us right now was an unwelcome one. When my shaft glistened, I squirted more on my fingers and slowly pushed one finger inside him.

"Damn, you're eating that," I said as I pumped my finger. "I'm going to give you another finger. Remember, wait until my cock is inside you, then you can come."

Embry hummed, his legs were quivering as he strained to keep his orgasm at bay.

After working his hole until it took three fingers, I carefully removed them and Embry whined so beautifully.

"Don't worry, I'm going to give you what you want."

I hovered over him, one arm rested beside him the other guided my cock into his very needy and very slick hole.

"Oh god," Embry moaned, and I wanted those words on my tongue. As I pushed into him, I swallowed his sounds with my lips and devoured his need.

My slow pace only lasted a few moments before I was slamming into him. Embry's bound hands gripped the ornamental piece he was tied to. With his head pushed back, his neck was exposed, and I couldn't help but to lick the sweat that dripped down.

"Mal," he whispered, and then his entire body froze as his orgasm swept through him. I rode him through it only to meet my own climax, too.

I could only hear the pulse in my ears and Embry's heavy breathing. I rested for a moment, knowing I had to release him and provide aftercare.

As I sat up and looked into his eyes, I saw a peace that had never been there. Even when I first met him he wasn't this relaxed, this content.

I slipped the restraints off, happy to see they only left minor pink rings.

"I'm going to get a cloth and some lotion, clean you up, and hold you for as long as you need me to, okay?"

Embry graced me with a serene smile and simply said, "Green."

I went to the bathroom as fast as I could, cleaned myself off, got a washcloth, lotion, and a dry towel. Embry was still in the same spot I left him in, and when I sat on the bed and began cleaning him, he hummed. It wasn't a tune, it was just a sound from deep inside him. When he was clean and dry, I took his hands in mine and applied lotion around the pinkish marks.

With Embry all cleaned and the lotion applied, I placed the towel and cloth on the floor and moved around the bed. I slipped in, pleased when Embry rolled into me. He squeezed me across my midsection and within moments, he was asleep.

A part of me wanted to ask him how it was for him. Did he feel freer? Did it work? Would he do it again? But grilling Embry right now would be foolish. I'd done enough research to know I had to wait until he was ready. One thing Embry and I had was excellent communication. Come morning, he'd have no trouble telling me exactly what he thought of all this.

With the moon peeking through the curtains, giving off a muted glow, I held my heart in my arms and drifted off to a peaceful sleep.

CHAPTER EIGHT

Embry

I woke to the sound of light clinking. I cracked open my eyes, glad the sun wasn't pounding me in the face and carefully searched my surroundings. Ahh, yes the hotel. I remembered every amazing second of last night. Including snuggling into Malcolm, who wasn't in bed now.

Lifting my head I saw why. He stood in just a pair of jeans and was fixing what appeared to be breakfast. I grabbed my glasses from the bedside table to get a better look. *Oh yeah, that ass.*

"Morning." My voice was rough which was typical of the morning.

Malcolm spun around, his hair was still mussed up from sleep, but he smiled like he was already awake and ready to start the day. "Morning. How're you feeling?"

I sat up more and glanced down at myself. I wasn't sore, not even my wrists. I slept amazingly well in the strange bed, and I felt no shame or regret… no frustration, anger, or stress.

"Better than I've felt in a long time, Mal."

"Yeah?" His brows shot to his hairline like he was flipping excited.

"You were right. That was…"

Mal walked over to the bed and sat beside me. "Was what?"

I wasn't sure I could articulate the feelings and emotions. How was one to describe the state I was in last night. The freeing sensation like I was— "It was like I was flying."

I didn't realize Mal's smile could stretch any wider, but it did. "Does that mean you're not going to be planning our vacation next year?"

A laugh bubbled out of me thinking of our deal. As much as I hated losing, I hated lying too, so it was one thing I'd never do. Especially to the man I loved. "Yes, Mal, that means I won't be planning our vacation."

His booming laughter made me jump for the longest time, but not anymore. Not for years now. Years. This man with his free spirit, beautiful smile, huge heart, and selfless soul, loved me. No matter what. My family wouldn't love him, and I couldn't stop loving him. I didn't even want to try, because a life not loving Malcolm was no life I wanted to live.

Malcolm went back to setting up our breakfast while I went into the bathroom to get ready for the day. Mal had a set of clean clothes folded on the small counter in the bathroom and all my toiletries together. I smiled as I turned the shower on.

As I quickly washed my hair and body, I thought about how Mal felt the night before. Familiar and yet new. He'd touched me a million times. Kissed me more than I could count, but last night was like some sort of restart. I felt refreshed and even chuckled at myself about how much I wanted to do it again soon.

When I came out of the bathroom, Malcolm was sitting waiting for me. "I got you two eggs over easy, bacon, hash browns, and we can share the pancakes."

That was my exact order to perfection. "Thank you." I smiled and sat, inhaling the delicious aroma.

We ate in companionable silence. My mind was racing as it played the previous evening over and over. Malcolm was humming with each bite, something that often annoyed me, but I didn't seem to mind right now.

"Sorry," he mumbled when he caught me staring. "I know you hate when I do that."

He shrugged and I couldn't stop myself. "You can hum. It's who you are. I know you're that person who wants moments to be immortalized. Or you do it out of reflex." I chuckled. "Either way, it's you. And…" I sighed and took a moment to collect my thoughts before continuing. "I loved last night."

Mal's eyes widened and pure joy morphed over his face. "I did, too."

"I had no idea one night could shake me up like it did, in a good way, of course." I reached over and gripped Mal's hand. "I hate being stuck in my head. The place I went to last night was so peaceful, but most of the time, it's a tornado of work, my parents, us. Things I want to change but just don't."

"What about us?" he asked, concern glittering in his eyes.

"Marriage, Mal. We aren't and we should be."

He nodded, eyes never leaving my gaze. "I love our life, Em. I just wanted you to step out of the suffocating environment your head was in. Let's take this a step at a time."

Our conversation was cut off by the phone on the table ringing. Mal reached over to answer it.

"Hello?" I watched as he listened to whomever was on the other line.

"Thank you, Helen. Embry and I will go over right after breakfast." He hung up and turned toward me. "Foreman needs to see us at the shop about the car. Maybe it's all fixed."

Where yesterday that would have thrilled me, it wasn't so

wonderful now. The second it was fixed, we'd be heading to Florida and my parents.

"I'll push the cart out into the hallway. Want to grab my wallet and stuff? Helen said the mechanic is two blocks from here. We can take a morning walk."

"Sounds great." I smiled and went over to the bed to get our things. I wondered if Malcolm would be happy if I said we should stay here for Thanksgiving. Just him and me in this room. Did they even have room service on Thanksgiving? I didn't know nor did I care, I just wanted to stay in this cocoon of contentment. I knew the second I saw my parents that would pop, and I'd be all twisted up again.

"Ready?" he called from the door.

"Yeah." I handed him his stuff and we left.

We had about made it to the mechanic when my phone buzzed in my pocket.

"You answer that and I'll go talk to Foreman." Mal kissed my cheek and walked over to Foreman without me, which was fine since I would likely be unfamiliar with what the issue was with the car. The phone buzzed again, and I looked and saw it was my mother.

"Morning, Mother."

"Good morning, Embry dear. I was calling to see if you'd heard anything?"

"We're actually walking into the mechanics now to find out." I watched as Foreman spoke with Mal. The car was on the lift and he was showing him something. "Oh, wonderful. I hope you'll be able to get on the road. Thanksgiving is tomorrow and I worry you won't be here."

I won't be here, not I'm worried you both won't be here. Mal never entered her thoughts, even after all these years.

"Let me go and see what's going on, and I'll call you in a little while." We said our goodbyes and I went over to the guys.

"So, how's it looking?" I asked and the look on both their faces said it wasn't good.

"Well, Em…" Mal sighed. "I have bad news."

CHAPTER NINE

Malcolm

THE SECOND FOREMAN TOLD ME HE HAD TO ORDER A PART I KNEW
we were screwed. There was no question Embry was talking to
his mother, and I already worried she'd bring him down again. I
had no idea how finding out we wouldn't be making it to Florida
for Thanksgiving would make him act.

"What's the bad news?" Embry stared at me and Foreman,
emotionless. This was placid Embry, the man who didn't show
you how he was feeling until his mind registered the appropriate
emotion.

"I was telling Malcolm here I had to order a part for the…"

Embry waved his hand dismissively. "I don't understand car
talk, so don't waste your time. Can you tell me when the part
should get here?"

"Well, so that's the thing." Foreman scratched his head, no
doubt nervous to tell Embry who was looking stern at this point.
"With Thanksgiving tomorrow, I won't be getting that part until
the day after, maybe two."

"So, we won't make it to my parents' for Thanksgiving?"

Embry flicked his eyes to me and I shook my head. "And I have to call her now and let her know this?" I nodded. "That's fucking great," he murmured. There was a tension in his eyes that I knew wasn't anger but instead, worry. Was it the fact that we weren't going or that he had to tell his parents?

"I'm real sorry," Foreman said. "I tried to get the part faster but nothing is open tomorrow, and I don't have the part here."

"It's fine, Foreman. I appreciate all you're doing. We'll head back to the hotel and see if Helen will be able to let us stay until after the holiday," I said.

"Oh, of course she will."

Embry had already walked outside the mechanics and started pacing. He wasn't on the phone, but he was certainly talking to himself. I approached him carefully, like one would a rabid squirrel.

"Babe?" I said, but he was in his head again.

"This isn't going to go over well. I'd love to think it would, but it won't. I'll have to listen to her go on and on, and then she'll try and make me go there without him. I won't do that; she's dumb to even think it."

"Em?"

"Maybe I should at least call and see if there are any seats to fly in tonight or tomorrow," he continued to himself.

"Embry Chaisten!" I spoke louder, and he finally stopped to look at me. "Stop."

"Mal, this is a disaster."

Placing both my hands on his shoulders, I took a deep breath. Then another. And another, until finally he was copying me.

"One thing at a time, Em. First, what exactly do you want to do?"

"It doesn't matter. I think we need to see if there are any last-minute tickets available and fly to my parents', and then fly back here after Thanksgiving when the car is fixed."

I hated that idea so much. "Is that what you want?" I placed a hand over his mouth before he spoke. "And don't say it doesn't matter, because to me it's the only thing that does."

He removed my hand and I was happy to see a small smile in place of the previous angry thin line.

"I don't know, honestly. But I think we should maybe see if there are tickets."

"Hmm. Okay. Let's go back to the hotel and see about the tickets. If there aren't any, I'll speak with Helen and see if we can stay until the car is fixed."

"Okay."

Once we got back to the hotel and were in our room, I started scrolling on my phone for any available flights. There were one or two spread out. When I asked Embry if he wanted to fly in without me, he shot me a look that said he'd rather be burned alive.

"There's nothing, then. It's right up there with Christmas as the worst day to travel."

He flopped on the bed with a groan. "I'm going to just call my mom and tell her. After she's done freaking out, I'll hang up and search for liquor."

I walked over and gently rested atop him with our lips inches apart. "Call her. Get it over with while I speak with Helen about staying here. When we're both done, let's see if we can't calm you down a bit." I tilted my head down enough I could skim my tongue over his lips.

"Mmm. Or we can not call her and barricade the door so Helen can't kick us out, and then you can help me calm down a bit."

I chuckled, glad when his blue eyes sparkled with mirth. "That some kind of fantasy, babe? I'll bring them all to life."

Lifting his head, he pressed his lips to mine. I returned it with fervor and feeling his cock hardening had me grinding against him.

"Jesus, Mal," he mumbled against my lips. "Fuck me."

I nipped and sucked his lips and was just reaching for his pants when his phone buzzed.

"You have to be kidding me." I reached into his pocket and saw it was his mom. "This is yours. I'll talk to Helen and then we can finish this." I winked and got up, making a show of adjusting myself.

"Calm that anaconda down," he joked, and loving his laugh, I decided to push the joke a little further.

"That's anacockda to you."

"No, Mal. It's never that. Never say that again. I'm erasing this conversation from my memory." He waved me away as he answered his phone. "Hello, Mother, I was about to call you."

I left him to it and searched for Helen. She was at the front desk and smiled when I approached.

"Good afternoon, Malcolm, how are you?"

"Well, been better but been worse, too."

Smiling, she closed the notebook she was writing in. "What's wrong?"

"Foreman told us we won't have our car until after Thanksgiving. It needs a part and while he ordered it, he won't get it until after."

She nodded. "I was afraid of that."

"So, I came down here to see if there was anyway Embry and I could extend our stay with you?"

She pulled the notebook back to her and opened it. "I don't see why not. How about I mark you for three days, and if it's still not fixed by then, we'll figure it out."

"Thank you so much, Helen. You've been a lifesaver."

She chuckled and wrote us into her book. "You're a charmer."

"One more question for you. Is there a place I can take Embry for Thanksgiving, or maybe even make him dinner?"

The expression she wore was adorable. It was like I said the most preposterous thing in the world. "Oh heavens, no. I live on Cranberry Lane, a few blocks from here. Dinner will be on the table around four. I have tons of food. You and Embry can come to my house. I insist."

"Oh, Helen. That's so nice of you but…"

"Hush. I won't hear of it. There's nothing open so it's too late to buy anything for dinner. Now, I won't hear more of this. Go upstairs and tell Embry that you'll be coming to my home for Thanksgiving." She pointed toward the elevator.

"Helen, I just…"

"Nope. Go."

"I don't think…"

"You're still here. Go. I have work to do, shoo." She grabbed her notebook and darted out of there faster than I thought her capable of moving.

I wasn't sure how Embry would feel about this, but I liked Helen and family was my thing, so I'd enjoy sharing a meal with hers. I had to hope he'd agree.

CHAPTER TEN

Embry

"You're far too quiet, Mother."

I told her everything, practically word for word, of what Foreman explained. I told her we searched for plane tickets to no avail. I even said as soon as the car was fixed we'd continue our drive down and celebrate Thanksgiving after. She hadn't said a word. If it wasn't for her heavy breathing, I'd think she'd hung up.

"Yes, Embry, well, Thanksgiving is ruined. I'm unsure what to say, exactly."

"What do you mean Thanksgiving's ruined?" The sound of my father's voice in the background had me bolting upright.

"Embry won't be able to make it..." I listened as she explained it all to my father, and he harrumphed and scoffed and all the things he did before he said something to monumentally piss me off.

"That's hogwash! There has to be one ticket he can get to fly in." And there was the stupid.

"He won't come without Malcolm."

There was silence again then a rustle and then, "Son, you're breaking your mother's heart."

"I'm not leaving him, Father. To suggest it is beneath your level of intelligence. You wouldn't leave Mother."

More grumbling. "This is different."

I knew I'd regret asking but what the hell. "How is this different?"

"Well, we're married and your parents. That's the difference."

The anger in the pit of my stomach boiled over at his words. "I'll give you the parents part, but that's it. And it's no more important than my reasons. As for the married part, do you really want to bring up a five-year-old argument?"

"Henry, give me the phone." My mother obviously heard my raised voice and wanted to extinguish this fire before it burned for another half a decade.

"Embry, dear. Your father just misses you and doesn't know what he's saying."

I should've probably left it, but I couldn't. "Do you agree, though?"

"That we're your parents? Of course." She chuckled.

"Do you feel Malcolm and I are more expendable and not as valid as you and Father are?"

Silence again.

"Embry, please. I don't want to do this over the phone."

"Do what? Answer a simple yes or no question the right way and end it, or the wrong way and not see me for another five years?"

I heard the door open and Malcolm enter.

"I have to go, Mother. I'm sorry *we* will miss Thanksgiving. I'll call when the car is fixed." This time I was the one to hang up.

The ache in my heart wasn't unfamiliar. I don't know why I thought five years would change them or that they'd even change at all.

"Hey." Malcolm stood in front of me as I sat on the bed. I leaned forward, resting my head against his stomach. His fingers running through my hair felt amazing, and I wrapped my arms around his waist hoping to keep him there.

"Just breathe, Em. I got you."

"It's never going to matter, Mal. To them. My loving you will never be seen as okay."

He scraped his nails against my scalp in the way that always relaxed me. He didn't say anything; he was just the presence I needed in that moment.

We stayed that way for what felt like an eternity. Malcolm moved slightly and pushed me back against the mattress.

"Stay right there, okay?" He kissed me and I watched as he went into the bathroom. When he came back out, he had a towel and the lotion he'd applied to my wrists last night.

"What are you doing?"

He smiled and placed the stuff beside me. "I'm going to put this towel on the bed, you're going to strip and lay on the towel, then I'm going to give you a special massage."

"How special?" I quirked a brow, interest pooling in my stomach, the ache almost completely gone.

"You remember your safe words?"

Oh! That kind of special. "Red for stop, green for go."

"Perfect. Now, do as you're told. Get naked and let's oil you up."

I didn't think, even if I was on fire, I couldn't have moved faster. I hopped off the bed and all but tore my clothes off, all the while loving Malcolm's booming laughter. When my ankle got caught in my pant leg, he simply sat back watching me work at getting naked.

The glint in Malcolm's eye when I climbed up onto the bed told me this wasn't going to be a typical massage. I knew he said special, and I was dying to find out what that meant.

"Gimme your glasses." Malcolm held his hand out and I placed my glasses in it. "I'm going to put the blindfold on, but I'm not tying your wrists. I want you spread out like a starfish, but I need you to just feel again."

I wanted that, to just feel. Not think or worry. Just be with Malcolm in that amazing bliss.

When the blindfold was placed, it was like a switch was hit. This was the moment that told me I was going to feel better. Malcolm was going to make it better. I wasn't sure what he got out of this, and I made a mental note to ask him. Then I felt the cool drops of the lotion on my legs and released a breath.

I focused on the feeling of his fingers kneading into my flesh, his breath right before his lips touched my skin. Soon my mind was slipping into that relaxing void. The painful ache was gone completely, and I was wrapped in Malcolm's everything. His scent danced over me and when his fingers brushed over my taint, a welcome shudder washed through me.

"I love how you feel," Mal whispered next to my ear. "Spread your legs wider."

Without hesitation, I did as I was told, his voice like an echo in my head calling to the wanton beast desperate to be free.

Mal's fingers pressed into my ass cheeks, and the air against my pucker told me how close he was to it. I never knew so much tension was in my ass. The thought almost made me laugh, but it froze in its place when I felt the swipe of Mal's tongue over my hole.

His hums vibrated through my body, sending waves of pleasure through every inch of me. He licked, sucked, and nibbled over my tender skin and all I could do was echo back my own hums and moans.

My cock was so hard, and I didn't become aware I was humping the mattress until Mal pushed me flat down on my lower back and growled not to move.

"Fuck," Mal said as he spread my legs even further. I didn't even realize my cock was peeking through until his tongue and mouth were dancing over the tip. He alternated from soft licks on my cock to lapping and sweet bites to my hole. I wasn't sure how much longer I would be able to hold back.

"Mal," I pleaded desperately.

"Yeah, baby." He sat back and the loss was almost too much. Suddenly I was flipped, and I didn't have a second to react before Mal was on me again and tearing off the blindfold.

"Come down my throat," he said and swallowed me down. Every nerve ending was reacting, I swear I felt Mal in my hair. Each suck was intense, and when my orgasm hit, I was zapped with an unspeakable amount of pleasure.

Slowly, I started to come to my senses and everything settled. I felt Mal get up like it was an earthquake.

"Stay," I whispered.

"I will, I just want to get cleaned up; that was hot."

I turned my head and saw Mal had come all over himself, and I let out a chuckle right before I fell asleep.

CHAPTER ELEVEN

Malcolm

By the time I came out of the bathroom, Embry was passed out. When I'd entered the hotel room and saw him practically vibrating with anger, the need to take it all away from him was my top priority. If he hadn't ended the phone call before I made it over to the bed, I was going to take the phone and end it for him.

His family never stopped hurting him. When Embry told me he didn't think he loved them, I couldn't fathom the thought. I loved my family immensely. But, my family and Embry's were so very different. My mom and dad loved Embry like he was one of their own. They acknowledged everything about him and never failed to surround him with all the things his own parents failed to do.

As carefully as possible, I lifted Embry up so I could get the covers out from under him. I slipped him under and then followed suit. He barely twitched, so I rested his head on my chest and breathed him in while he slept.

I had to tell him about Helen's offer for Thanksgiving tomorrow, but I needed to make sure he was in the right mindset. My hope was when he opened his eyes, he'd have let go of his rage and agree to the spontaneous Thanksgiving invite.

Embry only rested for about half an hour, and when he lifted his head and gazed at me with those beautiful blue eyes, I smiled —thrilled when he smiled back.

"Sorry I fell asleep."

"I'm glad you were relaxed enough to."

He huffed, kissed my chest and gave me the perfect opening for Helen's invitation. "So, what are we going to do for Thanksgiving?"

"Weeeellllll." I laughed when Embry's eyes widened. "Don't look so scared, I actually have a plan. Yes, a plan."

"Oh boy, things really are changing," he joked. "Tell me this big plan."

"Helen invited us to her home. She said everything closes down, and there's no other choice. So I told her I'd talk to you and see what you thought."

"You want us to go to a strange person's house and celebrate Thanksgiving with them?" He stared at me like I was crazy.

"Helen isn't a stranger."

"Uh." He sat up, the sheet pooled around his waist; it was a glorious sight. "My eyes are up here, mister." He smiled sardonically.

"Not even a little bit sorry for ogling you. Thirteen years and you still take my breath away, baby."

Embry's gaze softened and he hovered over me, inches from my face. "Okay, that was so sweet I will give you your weird Thanksgiving with strangers. But…" He placed his hand over my mouth before I got a chance to tell him how amazing he was. "If they kill me and stuff the turkey with my innards, I will be so very angry with you."

I chuckled and licked the palm of his hand. He rolled his eyes and wiped my spit on my cheek. "You're lucky I love you."

"I am."

He pressed his lips to mine and in that kiss, I knew Embry loved me just as much. He was a pain in the ass, all about planning and order, and he appreciated facts and proof. And yet, he stood up to his family for me. Me, who was the opposite of everything he was. I wasn't sure how we made it work, but we did.

"I have to ask you something." Embry straddled my waist, and I willed my cock to behave because the expression on his face was serious.

"What's up?"

"Last night, and a little while ago, what we did, that was amazing. I don't have words other than the flying feeling to tell you what it was like. You take all my burdens, pain, worries, and frustrations, and do away with them."

I furrowed my brows wondering where the question was. "I'm glad, Em."

"But, what do you get out of it?"

Placing my hands on his hips, I scooted up so I had my back full against the headboard. "Em, all those things you love about what we do and why, are the reasons I love them, too. I guess, like you, I can't really put it into words. I like freeing you. I've watched the chaos in your head for as long as I've known you, and I've always wanted to take it away. Watching you come undone just now and last night? Seeing how totally blissed out you were, and lost to all the things that tangle your mind… God, Em, that's an amazing feeling knowing I did that for you."

"Wow," Embry whispered and leaned into me. "I guess you're right, Mal."

I smiled so wide my cheeks ached. "I am? About what now?"

"Some surprises are wonderful."

We spent the rest of the day lounging in bed, kissing, making love, ordering Chinese—since at least it was open tonight—and watching whatever interested us on the television. I couldn't remember the last time Embry and I did nothing but be. We had no plans, and for me, that was how I liked it. Embry never once fidgeted or said he needed to call someone or check emails. He laughed at the cheesy comedy, broke all the fortune cookies until he found a fortune he agreed with, and cuddled like a pro. It was the best day I'd ever had.

"THERE HAS to at least be a florist or something open. We can't show up empty handed, Mal, it's rude." Embry was sitting on the sofa tying his shoe. He'd been a jittery mess all morning. I knew going to Helen's was going to be a hard pill for him to swallow for a few reasons. One, she was a stranger in his eyes; two, he was likely thinking about his family and what was happening there today; and three, we had nothing to bring.

"If this was a planned thing, I'd say yeah we should figure something out but, Em, this was a spur of the moment invitation. We can't break into a florist and get flowers. It's all closed." I stood by the door, coat in hand and waited for him to collect himself.

"It feels weird."

"It is weird, Em." I chuckled. "But weird can be fantastic."

He rolled his eyes and walked over to me. "At least try and block the butcher knife when Helen goes for my innards."

I gave him a peck on the lips and smiled. "I will get impaled for you."

"Dork." He grabbed his coat and followed me out of the hotel room. We had the address and the weather was working in our favor to walk there.

"She lives on Cranberry Lane?" Embry asked as we turned onto her street.

"Perfect, right?"

He narrowed his eyes at me. "It's too perfect… Serial killer perfect. Witch in Hansel and Gretel perfect."

"Shut up." I laughed. "There, that's her house." I pointed to the quaint red house with black shutters and a cobblestone pathway. She had pumpkins on the steps and burgundy and orange mums lining the walkway. It was picturesque.

"She's going to eat us," was the last thing Embry said before we rang the doorbell.

CHAPTER TWELVE

Embry

"HELLO, HELLO AND HAPPY THANKSGIVING TO YOU!" HELEN smiled at Mal and me when she opened the door. The aromas that assaulted us were heavenly. Turkey, gravy, pies, all of it, and I couldn't help but return the smile.

"Thank you, Helen, same to you." Mal reached over and gave her a peck on the cheek, typical Mal. I felt awkward and held out my hand.

"Oh, stop with that." She pulled me to her and hugged the stuffing out of me. She smelled of Shalimar and cranberry sauce and for a moment, I didn't feel so anxious.

"Let them come in, Helen, for turkey's sake," a joyful voice said.

"That's my husband, Barry. Come on in, boys."

We stepped inside and her house looked exactly like I assumed it would. Helen was a short woman with graying hair, green eyes, and a smile that made the dimple in her cheek pop. She was like everyone's grandmother and her home gave the same vibe. Tasteful floral couches, rose colored rug, pictures hung from everywhere, and the love radiating in this house was its own decoration.

"You must be Malcolm and Embry." I turned in time to not scream when a man, who I assumed was Helen's husband, took me in a bear hug. "I'm Barry, Helen's husband."

"Hey, Barry." Malcolm smiled into his hug and winked at me over Barry's shoulder. Helen and Barry were very much like Mal's parents. That didn't mean we weren't going to be dessert. I was being vigilant.

"Now, we can't eat quite yet," Helen said. "My daughter and her wife will be here in an hour, and my son had to run to the hotel to get me something. As soon as they get here, we can feast." She clapped her hands and laughed.

I was about to ask about her daughter and her wife when Helen's phone rang. "One second. Barry, why don't you get them some drinks? I'll get the phone."

"What can I get you, boys? I have cider, coffee, water, soda, and I believe beer. We can have the wine with our meal." He smiled.

"I'll have water, please," I answered.

"Cider, please."

Barry nodded and left us alone.

"They aren't so bad, huh?" Mal moved closer.

"So far, so good." I chuckled when he rolled his eyes.

"Excuse me," Helen said as she came into the room, her phone against her chest.

"Everything okay?" Mal approached her, but she waved him off.

"I think it is. Embry, do you know a Margaret and Henry?"

It felt like lead dropped into the pit of my stomach. "Those are my parents."

She nodded. "Okay, well my son is over at the hotel, like I

said, and they approached him. They said they flew in and are looking for you."

"They're here?" Mal's voice rang through the madness in my head. It was like a million bees buzzing.

"It appears so."

"Well, tell David to bring them over. We have more than enough food," Barry said as he came back into the living room with our drinks.

"Barry, hush." Helen inched closer to me. "Sweetheart, I can have David give them a room and later if you want…"

I appreciated what Helen was doing but I wouldn't hide. "Thank you, Helen. I can go back to the hotel to speak with them."

"Oh, don't be silly. Helen, tell David to invite them. Get a good meal in you first." Barry narrowed his eyes as if he was reading every emotion wiggling its way through me. "Something tells me it'll all go over better if you aren't by yourself. Am I right, Embry?"

"That's very kind of you, Helen and Barry. We don't want to bring anything here to your house on Thanksgiving," Mal said.

"David, tell Margaret and Henry they're celebrating Thanksgiving here, and they are welcome to join us if they wish." Helen paid no mind to what Mal or I said. She spoke to her son and then hung up and looked at me. "My daughter lit my Christmas tree on fire five years ago with all the gifts underneath. You can't possibly ruin a holiday like she has." She winked and went back into the kitchen.

"Here's your water." Barry handed it to me and I chugged it down, hoping it extinguished the horrific fire that was raging inside me.

"Babe?" Mal's hands gripped my arms and he pulled me into his chest, my now empty glass crushed between us. "What's going on in there?" He kissed the top of my head.

"Helen's daughter."

That seemed to shock him enough to pull back and his honey eyes stared at me. "Helen's daughter?"

"Yeah. She's married… to another woman."

It seemed to dawn on Malcolm what I was trying to say. "I want you to sit down right here and breathe for me, okay? I'm going to go talk to Barry and Helen. I'll let them know what they need to know. I don't want you worrying. Please, baby, can you sit here and I'll be right back?"

I must've nodded because he pushed me down to sit and walked out of the room with Barry to go talk to Helen.

Malcolm, Helen, and Barry had just entered the living room when the front door opened. A young man with a smile matching Helen's and eyes that twinkled like Barry's walked in.

"Happy Thanksgiving," he, I assumed was David, said.

"Happy Thanksgiving." Helen and Barry hugged him. Mal shook his hand, and I knew I needed to move, but right behind David was my mother and father. Neither looked excited to be here, and by the pinched look on my mother's face, she didn't approve of the décor.

"Hello and welcome, you must be Margaret and Henry?" Helen approached my mother, and if she saw the disgust there, she didn't let on. "I'm Helen, this is my husband Barry. You obviously met David, my son, and my daughter and her wife will be here any minute. Why don't I take your coats and you can visit with your sons while we bring coffee over?"

So many reactions ran over my parents' faces while Helen spoke. The fact her daughter had a wife was met with wide eyes, and when she referred to Mal and me as their sons, that was almost comical.

Like a tornado Helen swept in, she took coats, pushed her husband off to get coffee, and made David drop off whatever he had in his hands into the kitchen.

"Hello, Mother, Father." I nodded and stood.

"Happy Thanksgiving, Mr. and Mrs. Chaisten." Mal held out his hand and it was a movement he'd made a million times, but for some reason, right now, it felt all wrong. Helen and Barry embraced us… strangers. Mal's family embraced me. And my family? Thirteen years and never a hug or an ounce of respect for Malcolm.

"Happy Thanksgiving," my father grumbled and shook Mal's hand. My mother ignored him and came right over to me.

"Oh, Embry, Happy Thanksgiving." She smiled. "Your father's friend was able to work some magic and got us tickets to fly here and surprise you for Thanksgiving."

A part of me knew I should be grateful they did all this for me, but as I saw Mal over my mother's shoulder, looking over the pictures Helen had up of family, being utterly ignored by my parents, I wasn't grateful. I was resentful.

"Mother, how about pretending Malcolm is here and wish him a Happy Thanksgiving."

As if my mother was shocked by Malcolm's presence, she turned and chuckled. "I'm sorry, Malcolm, Happy Thanksgiving." She then turned back to me shutting him out once more. "Now, Embry, we were able to make a reservation at a wonderful place just forty-five minutes from here. They're open for the holidays. How about we go and have a lovely Thanksgiving dinner?"

I took a step back and scoffed. "Mother, Malcolm and I were invited here for Thanksgiving and we accepted. I'm not backing out."

"You had no issue backing out on us, though," my father said, which earned him a glare from my mother.

"We made the reservation for four, Embry. Malcolm is welcome, too."

Again, I knew I should be grateful, but she said it in such a way like she thought she'd done me a favor. I didn't get to respond before the front door opened once more and a boisterous voice sang through the air.

"Happy Turkey Day, blood relatives…" the person speaking saw me, Malcolm, and my parents standing there and quickly added on, "… and hopefully not murderers who killed and ate my blood relatives."

There was nothing to say to that, so I began laughing.

CHAPTER THIRTEEN

Malcolm

AFTER HELEN'S DAUGHTER, BEATRICE—*BUT CALL ME BIRDIE*—
arrived with her wife Jennifer, things got a little chaotic. Embry's
parents wanted him and me—really, just Embry—to come to
dinner with them, but it was as if Helen knew their game and
started complimenting Margaret on her clothes and Henry on his
tie, and the next thing we knew, we were all sitting around a
dining table filled with food.

I sat beside Embry thankfully, but his mother was to his left
and his father directly in front of him. I had to laugh when Birdie
opted to sit right next to Henry and said, "Thanks, Pops," when he
handed her the mashed potatoes. He turned as red as the cranberry
sauce.

"So, tell me, Birdie, what is it you do for a living?" Margaret
asked as she passed on the green bean casserole.

"I'm a tattoo artist up in Jersey, actually. Jen and I moved up
there about two years ago when she was offered a position in a
fancy-shmancy law firm." She winked at Jennifer who was on the

other side of me. It was interesting that they opted not to sit beside each other, but I had a feeling there was a reason for that.

"Oh, are you a lawyer?" That perked Henry's interest, and if Birdie was upset to be overlooked for her occupation, she didn't let on.

Jennifer smiled as she spooned some stuffing onto her plate. "I am. I worked down here for a while, even went to school here. When I got the offer to be a partner in a firm in New Jersey, I couldn't pass up the opportunity since it was in the field I wanted to work in most."

"Oh, and what is that?" Henry asked as he ate a forkful of potatoes.

"LGBT Rights."

He choked. Birdie began patting his back… it went downhill from there.

"Oh my word, is he okay?" Helen asked as she got up and ran toward the kitchen. "I'll get some water."

"Father, stop panicking," Embry shouted over everyone else.

"It's mashed potatoes, so it should slide right down, but it looks like it went down the wrong pipe," Barry said as he moved to Henry's other side.

"It's all one pipe," Margaret argued.

"No, there are two, as a matter of fact," Helen said as she came behind Henry to give him the water.

"But it goes to the same place." Margaret's attention was on Helen now. Henry was calming, but he was still coughing.

"Drink, Henry," I said.

"If it's in his trachea then no, it won't go to the same place, Margaret. That's why he's coughing, so it will go back to his esophagus." Helen was getting angry for the first time, and I knew first-hand Margaret had the ability to make a nun swear.

"How would you know? You run a hotel."

"I was a nurse for thirty years before I opened my hotel."

Margaret had the decency to look embarrassed, and Embry smiled, almost like he was proud of Helen.

They went back and forth long after Henry calmed down. Margaret and Helen were going at it and when I turned to Embry. I thought he'd be getting upset or stressed, but he wasn't. He was eating his food, paying them no mind. *Was he broken?*

"I question your opinions, Helen."

David, Helen's son, stood then and said, "You're a guest in our home and upsetting my mother. How about you sit down and be thankful we haven't kicked you out."

"Excuse me?" Margaret shrilled. "Henry, are you hearing this?"

He was trying to take deep breaths and regain control of his functions, but he nodded.

"Embry, I won't sit here and listen to this, we're leaving."

Embry scoffed. "Technically, you're standing not sitting, and I'm good here, but you can go if you'd like."

"Babe, you okay?" I whispered to him.

"Mal, I'm having a great meal. Is something wrong with me that I just don't want to deal with my parents?" He looked concerned and yet resigned at the same time.

"No. Just sit there and enjoy your food." I leaned into him and gave him a kiss. And that was the moment it went from chaos to madness.

"Oh, don't do that at the table, I'm eating," Henry said through a raspy voice.

"What's wrong with giving your loved one a kiss?" Birdie asked.

Margaret glared at Helen but sat back down.

"Nothing." Henry shrugged. "But this is the issue I have with the gays. They shove their beliefs down our throats. Make us see it. I don't deserve that."

Rage boiled in my stomach. I was about to rip into him when

movement beside me caught my attention, and the next thing I knew, Henry was wearing a spoonful of mashed potatoes across his face.

Everyone froze. It was silent aside from the plop of mashed potatoes that slid off Henry's face and onto his lap.

"Embry?" Henry asked. "Did you throw mashed potatoes at my face?"

Embry popped a piece of turkey in his mouth, cocked his head to the side and laughed. "I sure did."

"What ever has gotten into you?" Margaret asked.

"Let's see." Embry's brow bunched. "Mal got all up into me last night. It was wonderful, by the way."

"Oh that's disgusting, Embry," Henry yelled as he wiped his face. "No one wants to hear that on Thanksgiving."

"No one wants to hear your hate speeches either, but that didn't stop you," Jennifer said beside me.

"Hate speech?"

"You're aware my daughter is a lesbian married to a woman, and your son is in love with a man and they've been together for over a decade, right?" Barry asked, anger was simmering beneath his calm features. "You say you hate how the gays shove their agenda down your throat with a simple kiss. Well, you're shoving your hateful agenda down ours."

"Freedom of speech," Henry argued.

"Freedom of expression," Jennifer went back at him.

Barry shook his head and placed his napkin down. He turned toward me and Embry before speaking. "Before Birdie and David were born we had another son. His name was Frankie. If he were still alive today, he'd be close to thirty-seven. He died when he was seventeen. The second he was born we knew he was special. He loved to sing in the shower, wear Helen's perfume, dance in her heels, design gorgeous dresses he swore he'd create one day. Birdie and David didn't get the seventeen years we did with Frankie, but they got enough to feel his death."

I wasn't sure what to say. I knew there was a big reason Barry was telling us this, and I was glad when Henry and Margaret kept their mouths shut.

"He was walking home one night after stopping at a fabric store. He wanted to start seeing if he could make those dresses. He got a job and saved every penny for those fabrics and a sewing machine. He got jumped by five guys that night. They beat him so badly, wrote horrible words on his body with his own damn blood, and left him there to die."

I heard Margaret gasp and there were sniffles around us, but I couldn't look. I was drowning in the pain that had taken residence in Barry's eyes.

"He was on life support for three weeks. He was completely brain dead, but we couldn't pull the plug. It felt like we were giving up on him. But we knew that wasn't how he wanted to live. Letting him go was the hardest decision we ever had to make." Barry turned his head and stared right into Margaret's red-rimmed eyes.

"I don't know if Frankie was gay and I don't care. I knew he was a light and he was someone who wanted to bring joy to the world through fashion and music. I know five men had an agenda and chose to snuff out Frankie's light. I know I'd give my last breath for him to walk this earth again. And I know that while you aren't using your fists or feet to hurt your sons, you sure are destroying their light." Barry stood and I wanted to go to him, but I just waited.

"I'm sorry to dampen Thanksgiving, but I can't sit here anymore and listen to two parents, who have amazing boys here who just want to be loved, treat them like their love shouldn't exist." He nodded to me and Embry. "You're always welcome here, boys. Now, if you'll excuse me."

CHAPTER FOURTEEN

Embry

THERE WAS A LONG SILENCE, AS IF EVERYONE WAS TRYING TO figure out what to say or do. I was so embarrassed by my own family that I had to say something.

"Mother, Father, I think you've done enough damage. You've disrespected Helen, Barry, and their children on a day we should be thankful. Perhaps it's time you said goodbye and went back to the hotel."

I felt Malcolm squeeze my knee under the table, a silent show of support once again.

"Thank you, Embry," Helen said. "While this has been upsetting, I would be happy to have us all finish eating. Give Barry some time and he'll return." I knew she was hurt, and there was no hiding how the absence of her son was affecting her. I didn't want to argue anymore and ruin the evening further, so I let Helen have her bravado and nodded.

No one said anything else that would spark an argument. After dessert, my parents said they would be going back to the hotel and would see us in the morning. When my mother hugged me, I wasn't sure what to do. It wasn't that she never hugged me, but I could count on one hand how many times in my life she had.

"I'm sorry if I upset your holiday," Barry said to me after my parents were gone.

"You didn't, Barry. I'm so sorry for your loss. That's a horrific thing to have to endure. Frankie sounded like an amazing person."

He smiled brightly. "He was." I looked over his shoulder to where Mal was talking with Birdie and David. "When Birdie told Helen and me she liked girls, I told her that was lovely. I could never not love my children, and I'm heartbroken you've felt that pain from two people who should love you unconditionally."

"Oh, Barry." I shook my head. "Sometimes I think Mal was made for me. He makes up for all the abandoned hugs, cuddles, kisses, and love. I'll spend the rest of my life with that man and drown in his affections."

Barry scratched the back of his neck looking uncertain. "Can I ask you a question, Embry?"

"Of course."

"Well, can I ask why you and Mal aren't married? I mean I don't mean to pry, it could be you don't care for that sorta thing but…"

"No, we do. I do. It was my parents." I chuckled darkly. "Today was the first time I'd seen them in five years. Last time, we fought when I said Malcolm and I wanted to get married. While I stood up for him and told them I loved him, I never followed through on marrying him. I regret that."

Barry laughed loudly, garnering the attention of everyone. He leaned in and whispered to me, "No time better than on the day to be most thankful."

"Marry him today?" I whispered back.

"No, ask him. Make him a June groom." Barry winked and I laughed softly. In that moment, I didn't want to do anything but get on one knee and ask Malcolm to marry me.

Barry must've seen something in my expression because he chuckled and moved aside. Malcolm smiled at me, curiosity twinkled his eyes.

"You okay, Em?"

I didn't wait another second, right there in Helen and Barry's living room after the most insane and emotional Thanksgiving ever, I got down on one knee.

"Malcolm…"

"Em, what are you doing?" He was still smiling, and I knew he knew, but maybe he didn't believe what he was seeing.

"You said to me the other night seeing was believing, so you took away my sight, made me feel you. God, Mal, I feel you even when I'm not near you. You're in every stupid post-it note you leave for me and every, *oops I forgot to gas up the car*. You're in every surprise and joke. Now I want you to see. See and believe I love you more than anything and on this day, the day to be thankful, I want to ask you to be my husband forever. To see, feel, and believe with me until we are old, gray, and crotchety. Could you do that, Mal, could you marry me?"

I saw Birdie silently clap behind Mal's shoulder, and I felt her excitement, but for some weird reason, I was nervous. Did I wait too long? Would Malcolm think I was overly emotional after my parents' tirade? Would he…

"Yes, Embry. I'll marry you a hundred times."

I flipping giggled. When I stood, he swept me into his arms. Against his neck I said, "One time will suffice."

A pop that sounded a lot like champagne drew our attention. Helen stood there, flutes in hand, laughing. "That's how you close down Thanksgiving!"

Malcolm and I spent the next hour with Helen and her family drinking champagne and listening to how Birdie asked Jennifer to marry her. Barry and Helen's story was very traditional. David was grilled on his single status but said he hadn't found the right girl to settle with, but he was young enough and in no rush.

On the way back to the hotel, Mal and I walked hand in hand. There was a winter chill in the air and the promise of snow. I hoped it would at least hold up until we got back home, driving in the snow was a bitch and I really didn't want the Land Rover breaking down again, even if Mal felt he could handle the slippery roads.

"So, you going to tell your parents you proposed to me?"

I chuckled and kicked an acorn down the sidewalk. "I was thinking tomorrow at breakfast I'd let them know. A huge part of me doesn't feel like they deserve it, but then the part of me that's been growing these past two days tells me I want them to know. To know I love you regardless of their views. They can make memories with us or spend the rest of their days wallowing in the stale memories they've had all these years."

"Whatever makes you happy, Em. Whatever you decide with your parents, I'll support."

"I know." I lifted his hand to my lips giving it a quick kiss.

"My parents are going to be so excited," Mal laughed through his words. "Oh man. But I want to tell them in person. I've got to see my mom's face."

"You got it."

When we got back to our hotel room it was close to ten at night. I felt tired but awake, so I went to the bathroom and decided to get a bath going.

"You up for a bath?" I asked Mal as he began divesting himself of his clothes.

"Sounds perfect."

It was a bath full of kisses, hugs, lots of rubbing, and laughter. We washed each other, and Malcolm was being silly and made a ring out of the suds. I asked him if he wanted me to get him a ring, but he said he'd rather wait until we got married and have matching ones. When we got out and dried ourselves, I could see the exhaustion on Mal's face. I pulled the sheets back and on the nightstand, I saw the feather tickler.

"You never used this, did you?" I asked and he shook his head. "Well, I can't wait to see what you do with it."

I crawled over him, pecking his lips before settling on my side of the bed.

"You don't want to think something up with it?" Mal asked as he removed my glasses.

"Nah, I sort of like it when you take control of things in the bedroom." I couldn't help but waggle my brows. "Who knew, right?"

He chuckled and gathered me in his arms. I closed my eyes, breathed in his scent, and fell into a deep sleep.

CHAPTER FIFTEEN

Malcolm

I felt the most glorious suction around my cock. I was in that space between sleep and awake where I knew it was Embry, but I also swore Guns N Roses was playing in our bedroom.

I opened my eyes a crack and saw a mound under the sheets bobbing up and down. I placed my hand on top of Embry's head and when he hummed, I thought I'd see about turning this into something more than a morning blowjob.

"Mmm, yeah, suck my dick," I growled. Embry halted for a moment but went right back to it. There was no way I was going to hold on long but pushing Embry was something he needed, liked, and to be honest, I loved.

"All the way down on it." I pushed his head down until he had my whole cock in his mouth. I knew he could swallow me whole, but I also knew by doing this he couldn't safe word.

"I'm gonna hold you down on my cock, force you to take it until I say you can breathe. You won't be able to safe word, so tap my leg if you want to stop. Got me?"

Em slipped my cock out of his mouth and tore the covers off

our bodies. His smile was gorgeous and he had a playful gleam in his eyes. "Yeah, Mal. I got you."

"Good." I gripped his hair and pushed him back onto my cock.

I was so fucking hard I was going to shoot any second. "Squeeze my base, I don't want to come yet."

He did and lapped at my balls for a few seconds, giving me a little time to calm down. I liked having my balls licked, a lot, but Embry's suction was orgasmic… literally.

"Back on my dick and don't get off it till I say." I held my cock and fed it to him. Once he sucked me in, I put both hands on the side of his face and pushed up and face fucked him. His blue eyes trained on me the whole time were an added bonus.

"You want my come, baby?" He hummed in response. "Yeah. I'm gonna give you all of it and you're gonna swallow it all. If you don't, if even a drop slips past your gorgeous lips, there'll be no coming for you until I say."

Embry's eyes widened but nothing more. He was loving this.

"'Kay, baby, open wide."

I pounded into his mouth and when I started coming, he closed his lips tight and drank me down… Every. Single. Drop.

"Holy hell." My legs relaxed and Embry pulled off my dick.

"Holy hell is right. Damn, Mal, that was hot."

I crooked my finger and he crawled up my body. I gathered him in my arms and kissed him. I tasted myself and loved every second of it. Feeling his hardness against me, I knew I had to reward him for being so good.

"Straddle my face and gimme that pretty dick of yours."

He didn't have to be asked twice. He had his cock down my throat in seconds. I squeezed his cheeks and pushed him deeper down my throat until I felt the burst of come. He tasted so sweet, and I held on until he was completely spent.

We didn't rush out of bed and Embry didn't mention his

parents, who I knew would be messaging him to meet downstairs for breakfast at any minute. I thought about what my family was doing at home. It was Black Friday so no doubt my mother was home already after tackling people for the best savings. I missed them at Thanksgiving, but I didn't miss her dragging me with her to the mall to lug heavy shit.

"Why haven't you used the feather tickler?" Embry asked as he ran his fingers through the hair on my chest.

"Oh, I'm gonna, just haven't decided when, where, or how." I chuckled. "Why, you eager?"

He shrugged. "I might be."

I was loving this side of Embry. In all the years I'd known him, he was never so carefree. I was so glad he agreed to go into Ace's Wild with me a few days ago. I was about to mention we go back there before we left when his phone vibrated on the nightstand.

"Ugh." He reached over me and grabbed it. "My mother texted us an invite for breakfast downstairs."

"Both of us?"

He nodded. "I'll tell her one hour. I'm not going to rush." He placed the phone back down and sprawled on top of me. "I want to take a nice long shower with you before we face the firing squad."

"Baby." Lightly, I caressed his cheek. "We don't have to go down there at all. You owe them nothing."

His smile made my whole body tingle all the way to my toes. "I know, but after yesterday, hell, after the last few days, I feel like a new person. I want to tell them I'm marrying you and spending forever with you. They'll have to decide on the spot if they're going to be a part of our life or not. None of this having to think about it shit."

Holding his head in place, I lifted up and kissed him with everything I had. I poured every ounce of love I had for this amazing man into that kiss until he moaned and writhed against me.

"Let's go take that shower, shall we?" I said, and he bounced off me and ran to the bathroom.

"Last one in has to sit next to my father at breakfast."

Oh hell no! I tried to beat him, but he had one hell of a head start.

"It seems the breakfast here is buffet only," my mother said with a shrug. "Hopefully it's fresh and not breathed on."

"Wow, yeah okay. I'm getting my food, then." I got up unable to listen to it anymore. I hoped after last night they'd have seen some light, but I had a feeling this wasn't going to go as Embry planned.

"Morning, Malcolm," David greeted me when I was plating eggs.

"Hey, David. I didn't think I'd be seeing any of you today."

"Mom and Dad take the day after Thanksgiving off, and Birdie and I handle the hotel." He was filling the sausages up when Embry came up beside me.

"I figure we drop the bomb halfway through breakfast."

David chuckled. "Gearing up to tell the folks about the wedding?"

Embry nodded. "Yeah, I figure halfway so if it goes poorly we'll have enough food in us to get by. If it happens to go well by some miracle, I'll only have to endure their fake happiness for half a meal."

"Why not just finish breakfast, then tell them?" David asked.

"Because I'm equal amounts hungry as I am wanting to run away from this whole thing."

"Well, good luck with your eating compromise." David left us to fill our plates. When we returned, Henry and Margaret got up to get their food.

I would have laughed at how fast Embry was eating if I wasn't so eager to get this over with, too.

"So, tell us when you think you'll be able to leave here?" Margaret sat down with her plate of food and began fixing her tea, staring at us nervously.

"I'll be calling Foreman after breakfast to see. I suspect a couple more days since the part is going to be delivered today or tomorrow, but I'll know more later." I shoveled the last of my eggs in my mouth hoping to stave off any further answers.

"And then what do you boys plan on doing?" Henry asked.

"We'll drive back home. School opens back up on Monday, so I have to have him home by then. Which, yeah, I'm not sure how, but we'll figure it out." I shot him a wink and a small smile was the most I was able to get out of him.

"Ahh yes, school," Henry mumbled around a piece of toast.

Embry's fork clanged against his plate and I discreetly reached under the table to place my hand on his knee. A silent show of support.

"Mother, Father, I actually have something very important to tell you both." He closed his eyes and took a deep breath. When he opened them, he smiled so serenely I emulated it.

"What is it, Embry?" Margaret gave him her full attention.

"Last night I asked Malcolm to marry me and he gladly accepted."

Aside from the patrons in the dining room eating and talking, there were no other sounds. Margaret blinked owlishly and Henry stopped eating his bacon mid chew.

"We haven't set a date but maybe June." His blue eyes sparkled when he turned toward me.

"I think that's perfect."

CHAPTER SIXTEEN

Embry

"Can't you just go on the way you've been?" my father asked, and the perfect bubble I'd been in moments ago, looking into Mal's honeyed eyes, popped.

"Why should I have to when Malcolm and I both want to be married? Why couldn't you and Mother have gone about just living together and forgone a wedding?"

It was rewarding seeing the blush form on my father's rounded cheeks. "Well, that's…"

"Different, yes, so you've said." I released a breath and rested my napkin on my plate. "I want nothing more than for you both to give me your blessing and live this life with me and Malcolm. I know you'll say you need time to think about it, but I'm sorry, I'm not going to give it to you."

My mother's eyes widened. "Embry, you just sprung this on us."

"No, Mother, I didn't. Five years ago I told you this was what we wanted, and it started a war. In that time, the only thing that's changed is I love Malcolm even more. We will be getting married, it's a matter of: will you two be in our lives or is this goodbye?"

"Our flight leaves in three hours. I can't be thinking about any of this now." My father stood. "When everyone is settled at home, we can discuss this further."

"I think you misunderstand, Mr. Chaisten. Embry isn't giving you time. You've had plenty. Either bless this or say goodbye to your son." Malcolm squeezed my knee and I appreciated the anchor.

"I won't be rushed into such things. Come along, Margaret, we'll miss our flight."

He held his hand out to Margaret, but she just stared at Embry, an odd expression on her face.

"No, Henry," she whispered, and I watched as a tear slid down her cheek. "I think I'll catch a later flight."

"What?" he blustered. "There aren't later flights, this was a favor to get these tickets, we can't —"

She cut him off with a chuckle. "Then go ahead and take the flight." She looked up at her husband. "All night I tossed and turned thinking about Helen and Barry's son, Frankie. I dreamt that it was Embry on the ground beaten, dying. I woke in a sweat and as I stood in the shower I realized, while we haven't used fists to hurt our son, our words have been far more lethal."

She turned back to Malcolm and me and held her hands out to us. We took them, hesitantly. "I don't want to ever say goodbye to you, Embry. And I apologize to you both for the pain I've caused you. I can't say I'll change overnight, but I promise I won't hurt you anymore." She smiled at us both. "I happily bless this marriage."

I released her hand and in an uncharacteristic move, we both stood and hugged and cried and even laughed.

"You bless it?" Henry asked quietly. "Can we discuss this?"

"What's to discuss?" Mal interjected. "I love your son. I'll never let anything or anyone hurt him. I'll make sure his wants and needs are always met, and I have and will continue to put him above everything. How could you not want that for him?"

"I do want that for him I just…"

"Want it to be with a woman?" Malcolm finished my father's statement.

"Can you blame me for wanting my son to have an easier life?"

I was glad the two of them were keeping their voices down, but people were looking.

"Can we maybe sit?" I asked, glad when everyone complied.

"Don't you see the only ones that have ever made it hard for Embry are his own parents?" Mal asked softly. "If it wasn't him loving me, it was his job or where he chose to live. You never made him feel like his life was enough, and I've spent the last thirteen years showing him it's more than enough for me. I love Embry no matter what. If he quit teaching tomorrow and said he wanted to be a street performer, I'd buy him his first pair of tap shoes. That's how much I love your son."

I didn't even realize I was crying until I blinked and a tear fell from my eyes. You didn't live with someone for thirteen years and not know they love you, but the passion in Malcolm's words in that moment, coupled with what he'd opened my eyes to these last few days, made me almost suffocate in my love for him.

My parents sat stock still after Malcolm's gorgeous confession. My mother with a small, and slightly ashamed, smile on her face. She may have apologized and blessed our marriage and promised she'd be better, but that didn't absolve her of the years of hurt she'd put me through. My father was blinking at Mal like he had three heads but had the decency to look embarrassed.

I wasn't sure what my father was going to say, and I didn't get a chance to find out. Mal stood and held his hand out to me.

"Embry and I are going to speak with the mechanic, and we have some things to do today. We wish you both a safe flight home." He turned and offered my mother a smile. "Thank you, Margaret, you have no idea how much your words have meant to us. I wish words were enough sometimes, but now I think it's your actions that need to move mountains."

Without another word, Malcolm and I made our way out of the dining area and into the hotel lobby.

"I didn't want to give them an out to think about it," I said as we made our way toward the exit of the hotel.

"Em, I don't know what your father was going to say, but I do know your mother is likely laying into him something fierce right now. We aren't giving either of them time to think; we're letting them finally say to each other what I think they always wanted to." He winked then, and it shocked me to see the brightness in his expression.

"Looks like maybe you and I aren't the only ones to discover new tricks here in Vintage Ridge."

I laughed all the way out of the hotel, and we were halfway down the block before I realized we weren't going the direction of Foreman's.

"I thought we were checking on the car?"

He nodded. "We will, but I wanted to make a stop first." I was about to ask where when we rounded the corner and the Ace's Wild sign came into view. From where we stood we saw the big guy, Ace, on a ladder trying to tie the very large inflatable Santa to the roof. I wasn't sure how successful he'd be, but I wasn't going to say anything.

"Hello down there," Ace's voice boomed as we were about to enter.

"You be careful up there, big guy." I laughed when his eyes widened.

"You're adorable. I'm always careful. And it's Black Friday, so we have great sales. Have fun." He winked and went back to his, hopefully successful, hanging of the Santa.

CHAPTER SEVENTEEN

Malcolm

ACE'S WILD WAS IN DECORATION MODE AND THERE WERE SALE signs hanging everywhere. I tugged at Embry's hand and he dutifully followed.

"We haven't even used the feather tickler and you want more things?"

"Actually, no," I said, and he shot me the most adorable look. "We're going to walk around the store and you're going to list off things you'd be willing to try, and I'm going to tell you things I want to try. We're doing this because I think we found something within ourselves we didn't realize was there until this week."

"That's a good plan."

We spent the next hour walking the aisles talking about all the toys we saw. I was surprised about how many lube brands there were and even more shocked the store had books. Embry said it made sense since it was a good way to learn if you were curious and alone.

Wilder smiled as we meandered the aisles but never once made us feel like we had to buy anything. By the time we finally left to head over to the mechanic, Embry and I had discovered we maybe weren't as vanilla as we'd thought, and I was so excited to try new things in the future.

~

"I KNOW you boys are itching to get home and I do have a rush order in, but it looks like Sunday? I'll work Saturday to get it all fixed up but yeah, I'm sure sorry," Foreman said as he wiped sweat off his forehead.

"I sort of figured," I said as I eyed my Land Rover where it sat in the garage. At least it wasn't sitting outside. I turned to apologize to Embry, knowing he was going to miss school on Monday. "I'm sorry, Em. This is my fault."

He shook his head. "No, it's not. It's fine, there's nothing anyone can do. I'm sure I can explain everything."

The Embry I knew would have rolled his eyes and said something accusing me of my friend Zell doing this, or told me why flying was better, or something negative. This new Embry, this calmer one, was nice.

"You can always fly home. I'm sure you can get a flight today or tomorrow easily. I'll drive the car back."

This time he did roll his eyes. "No, Mal, we're seeing this crazy Thanksgiving adventure to the end together."

I chuckled. "You're sure?"

"I already texted my boss while Foreman was telling us the news."

Leaning into him I captured his lips, kissing him until he moaned and Foreman chuckled. "Okay, guys, well I think you all need to find a bedroom or something."

After one last kiss, I pulled back and smiled at the teddy bear of a man. "Thanks, Foreman."

We spent the rest of the day walking around the town, eating lunch, breathing in the crisp air. At no point did Embry's parents message him or call, and while I didn't want to face the music quite yet, I knew it was inevitable. We walked into the hotel and were greeted by Birdie.

"Hey, newly-engaged. How's ownership treating you?"

Embry and I both chuckled. "We had a great day, how are you?"

"Fine, fine. So, your lovely 'rents left a message for you. I guess they were going to call you but your mom was all, *no, I don't want to ruin their day*." She rolled her eyes and handed us an envelope.

"Thanks, Birdie."

We waited until we were back in the room and snuggled under the covers before opening the letter. With Embry's back to my chest I read over his shoulder.

Dearest Embry and Malcolm,

I stand by what I said this morning. I bless your union and promise to prove myself worthy of being a part of your life. I'm not sure if you will, but know if I can do anything to assist in the wedding, I will.

I don't know where your father is on any of this. After the two of you left, he didn't say two words to me. I was going to stay but realized it may be worse if I did. Please call me when you return home to let me know you're safe.

I'm so sorry for hurting you both and very much hope you give me time to make it up to you.

Love,

Mom

"Wow, she signed it Mom," Embry said through a thick voice.

"Time, Em. I can't blame you one bit for not trusting this. But find peace in knowing you have the control here. You can decide how worthy or not she is. As for your father? I don't know, just know I'm here for you."

"Mal?"

"Yeah, baby?"

He turned in my arms, his blue eyes glittering, his knuckles white as he clenched the letter. "I don't want the control. I always thought I did, but I'm not good at it. I don't want it now, tomorrow, ever."

Cupping his cheek, I smiled. "Sometimes we're forced to be in control. Your classroom is yours and no one can run it like you do, but I suspect that's not what you mean."

He nodded. "It's not, I mean this, us."

I knew what I had to do, what he needed from me, and what I craved. "Lay flat on the mattress, Em, let me take care of you."

Embry tossed the letter aside and rested on the mattress like a starfish. I had to hurry and move or get smacked in the face with how fast he moved.

"Remember your safe word?" He nodded, his blue eyes showed how eager he was. "I'm going to blindfold you and tie you up."

"Okay."

When his arms were tied to the ornate post on the bed and his eyes covered, I reached into the dresser for the feather tickler. I watched as Embry's chest rose and fell faster and faster in anticipation. When I lightly brushed the feathers over his rapidly hardening cock, he yelped, and I couldn't hold back my chuckle.

"Just feel, Em."

I barely touched his skin with the feathers, and the reaction was more than I could have dreamed. His back arched, his body shook with need, and his moans were beautiful. His cock was hard and when I took a taste of his pre-come, he whimpered.

"Mmm, damn you taste good. Might need another taste."

I loved how his breathing picked up and how his nipples

pebbled. His reaction to my words alone was enough to make me come.

"You don't come until I say you can, you understand?"

"I do, god, Mal, I can't."

"You will." I gripped his cock to stave off his orgasm, not enough to cause pain, just enough for him to know coming before I said so wouldn't make me happy.

"Count for me, Em. Let me hear you. From ten."

He took a deep breath and with a shaky voice began. "Ten, nine, eight…"

"Slower." I kept my grip on his cock as he counted.

"Seven, six, five."

"That's good." I leaned down and licked the head of his dick.

"Fuck, four. Shit. Three."

With my hand still wrapped around his shaft, I took Embry's entire head and gave it a few good sucks.

"Oh for… two." He was writhing, sweating, and I peered down his goose-fleshed body to his curled toes and smiled.

"One… One, Mal!" he shouted as I released my hand from his cock and swallowed him down.

He howled with great abandon and I relished in his taste as he came down my throat. As he caught his breath, I licked every drop and worked my way up his body, removing the blindfold and untying his wrists. He lay there like a spent man who was drained of everything but happiness and air.

"You doing good?" I asked as I wiped his sweaty bangs from his forehead.

"I'm amazing, Mal." He gazed at me, sparkling love and wonder. "You're amazing, Mal. I love you so fucking much."

Em wasn't one to curse, so hearing him unable to form anything besides them made me smile and I captured his mouth. We kissed for what felt like hours. He didn't protest when I swooped him up and carried him to the bathroom. He smiled when I placed him in the bubble-filled tub, and he hummed contently when I washed his body.

When we fell asleep in each other's arms later that night, I knew it wouldn't matter what Embry's parents did, Em and I were strong. What we had was unbreakable and forever.

CHAPTER EIGHTEEN

Embry

"Now I packed a basket for you, it's in the trunk with your luggage." Helen hugged me and Mal like we were never going to see her again.

"I bet it's delicious, thank you, Helen." Mal kissed her cheek and turned toward Barry. "Thank you for your hospitality and for the best Thanksgiving I've ever had."

"Most memorable, maybe." Barry chuckled and gave Mal a hug, and then me.

"Don't you all be strangers, now." Helen appeared teary and I hated that so much.

"Oh, Helen, if you think Malcolm and I aren't coming back here, you're crazy. Vintage Ridge holds more memories for us than any other place we've ever vacationed. Thank you for making this a place we will visit often and love forever."

That started another round of hugs, tears, and Birdie clapping, which got passerbys clapping, and suddenly everyone was applauding.

Malcolm and my road trip home was a lot less eventful, and

while I was eager to get home, the farther we got from Vintage Ridge the more my heart ached.

We were pulling into a motel, where we'd stay the night before making the last leg of our journey home, when I grabbed Mal's arm.

"I want to get married there," I blurted out.

He peered out the windshield, confused. "Here at the Red Roof Inn?"

A laugh burst out of me. "No, I want to get married in Vintage Ridge at that hotel. I want to go back there every year and remember how our lives changed there. It's magical, Mal, don't you feel it?"

He grabbed my hand and sandwiched it between his like he was praying. "It is a magical place and I'm so glad you want to get married there. I was going to ask if it was something you'd entertain, so of course I'm on board with it."

"Yeah?" Excitement bubbled in my belly.

"Hell yeah!"

"June?"

He was as giddy as I was. "Hell yeah!" he said again.

I was so happy I undid my seat belt and crawled over to him and straddled his lap, taking his face in my hands and kissing him breathless.

"Damn, baby, we need to check in. They'll see us," he spoke in between my kisses.

"Let them see."

His laughter vibrated through me. "What's gotten into you, baby?"

"Mmm, you will I hope."

He squeezed my ass and we sat like that, making out like a couple of randy teenagers, until a cramp in my leg had me pulling back.

"Let's take this inside."

He agreed and we took a few minutes to will our cocks down. The basket Helen had made for us was long gone and our stomachs were rumbling.

We ordered pizza, sat almost naked on the shitty bed, and planned our wedding. We were so excited to get back to Queens and tell Malcolm's family and call Helen and ask her if we could use her hotel. We were ecstatic.

"This is going to be a great wedding. Best anyone's ever been to." Mal laughed around a slice of pizza.

"Oh, you know something to make it the best, do you?" I tossed him a napkin when sauce dripped onto his chest.

"Oh yeah, I've got a lot of tricks up my sleeve." He waggled his brows and I fell into a fit of laughter.

One thing I'd learned was that my fiancé was full of new ideas and new tricks, and I was excited to spend the rest of my life discovering each one.

EPILOGUE

Seven Months Later
Malcolm

"IT'S SATAN'S ARMPIT HOT OUTSIDE," I SAID AS I CAME INTO THE room with my tuxedo in hand.

"Well, it's June, what did you expect?" My mom rolled her eyes as she took my suit and hung it up. "Go shower and then you need to hustle. You know Embry has probably been ready for four hours already."

"The wedding doesn't start for another two hours." But I said no more, I went into the bathroom to wash up.

Embry and I didn't do the not seeing each other the night before our wedding thing, but we'd agreed we'd part ways after breakfast and wouldn't set eyes on each other until the ceremony. So I moved everything over to my parents' room and let Embry stay in the beautiful suite Helen gifted us for the week of our wedding.

As I washed my body and made sure I was wedding-night worthy, I thought about the whirlwind of the last seven months.

Thankfully, Helen and her family were such a huge help we didn't have to take more than one trip to Vintage Ridge to get ready for the wedding.

Margaret Chaisten kept her promise to Embry and turned her words into action. There was a whole lot of silence from his father, but we all thought he'd come around. Then one morning in April, there was a knock on our door and there stood Margaret and four suitcases.

She told Embry she'd tried everything, and when Henry gave her an ultimatum him or Embry, she packed her bags and did the first spontaneous thing she'd done in her whole life. She left him to be closer to her son.

I knew it hurt Embry whenever questions about his father came up, but everyone around him made sure he felt our love and acceptance.

We opted not to have either of us walk down the aisle and enter at the same time from the sides. I knew my parents wanted to walk me down, but for all these years, even though my family supported us, so often it had been Embry and me against the world. We wanted to face this part of our lives at the same moment, together.

Through the last seven months we kept in touch with Helen of course, and surprisingly, Ace and Wilder. They were huge helpers as Embry and I navigated our new lifestyle. When we invited them to our wedding via Skype, Ace actually cried and Wilder just laughed.

Today was going to be the best day ever.

"Oh my god, Mal, save some water for the ducks!" my mother shouted through the door. I chuckled and shut off the water. I caught my reflection in the mirror as I dried off. I looked the same as I always did but my smile was wider. I was happy.

"Holy shit, Mal, move it or lose it."

"Jesus, Ma, I'm coming."

I shook my head and hurriedly dried off. With a towel around my waist, I walked into the bedroom to get dressed. I came to a screeching halt when atop the bed sat my soon-to-be husband. He wore a classic tuxedo and a mischievous smile.

"What are you doing here?" I whispered and went toward the bedroom door to make sure it was locked.

He chuckled. "How do you think I got in here? Your mom let me in, and she's giving us a few minutes before the ceremony."

I turned and bumped right into him. He gripped my towel and tugged.

"Mmm, this is better than the tux."

"Do we have time?" I asked as he ran his finger the length of my cock.

"Nope." He accentuated the P. "But that's not why I'm here."

"Oh, well, babe, if you're not here to get on your knees and suck my cock, can you stop making it grow? I gotta get into a suit that was tailored to me when I was flaccid."

He gathered up some pre-come and brought it to his lips before taking a step back. "I have a gift for you."

"You're killing me, Em, killing me."

He laughed and took something out of his pocket. "Here."

I took the rectangular box and opened it. Inside was a sleek black oval thing with a button. "I don't…" I clicked the button and Embry hummed. Then I heard a different kind of hum. "Oh no way, is this?"

He nodded. "I'm sort of freaking out here and there. I remembered what Ace said to us about finding ways to keep things calm when in public, and I thought, when things get too hectic you could…" He gestured to the small remote that was connected to the butt plug my soon-to-be husband clearly had in his hole.

"Jesus, Em."

"Yeah. Happy Wedding Day, Mal." He stood on his toes and gave me a chaste kiss. "See you out there." He shot me a wink and was gone.

Yeah. Our life was going to be the best!

The End

OTHER BOOKS BY DAVIDSON KING

Haven Hart Series:

Snow Falling

Hug It Out

A Dangerous Dance

From These Ashes

Snow Storm

Triple Threat

Raven's Hart

Collaboration with JM Dabney

The Hunt

ACKNOWLEDGMENTS

Big thank you to ALL the authors involved in the Ace's Wild Series! It's been an amazing ride and they've truly been outstanding.

Thank you to my beta and editing team: Annabella, Jenn, Lori, Steph, and Anita you make my words sparkle. And thank you to Morningstar Ashley for the gorgeous cover and to Luna David for the flawless formatting.

As always, none of this would be possible without the love and support of my family. I love them all and am a better person because of them.

ABOUT THE AUTHOR

Davidson King, always had a hope that someday her daydreams would become real-life stories. As a child, you would often find her in her own world, thinking up the most insane situations. It may have taken her awhile, but she made her dream come true with her first published work, Snow Falling.

When she's not writing you can find her blogging away on Diverse Reader, her review and promotional site. She managed to wrangle herself a husband who matched her crazy and they hatched three wonderful children.

If you were to ask her what gave her the courage to finally publish, she'd tell you it was her amazing family and friends. Support is vital in all things and when you're afraid of your dreams, it will be your cheering section that will lift you up.

If you'd like to join my newsletter or find me around the internet click on my Linktree and a list of all my links will be there: linktr.ee/davidsonkingauthor

www.ingramcontent.com/pod-product-compliance
Lightning Source LLC
Chambersburg PA
CBHW052059150726
48002CB00002B/959